# SEAL's Obsession

## Take No Prisoners Series

*Elle James*

D1473963

**SEAL**'s Obsession

# **SEAL**'s Obsession

Tasked with finding and eliminating the source of terrorist pirate activities off the coast of Honduras, SEAL TEAM 10's Jack Fischer "Fish" goes undercover as a deck hand on a floating medical boat where he finds himself protecting and falling for the beautiful doctor who runs the show.

Devastated by an auto accident that took the lives of her husband and baby daughter, Dr. Natalie Rhoades, has dedicated her life to helping people who don't have access to good healthcare through her nonprofit floating medical boat. When she finds herself and her crew the target of a leftist guerilla group, her new deckhand proves resourceful.

Jack and Natalie fight to provide the care needed to the underprivileged while battling an attraction neither thought possible as it heat intensifies in Central America.

# From the Author

I'm dedicating this book to my 92-year-old neighbor who spent 26 years in the Navy, was a fighter pilot who made over 600 carrier take offs and landings and fought during WWII and Korea. He's an amazing man. Thank you for your service!

Escape with...
Elle James
aka Myla Jackson

# Chapter One

"I wonder what you have to do to retire in a place like this?" Navy SEAL Corpsman Jack Fischer cut the engine on the jet ski, letting it slide across the crystal clear water and up onto the white sands of the beach.

"You have to either belong to a cartel or pay the cartel to protect you," said a voice through the earbud. Swede, the computer guru and all-around electronic techie on SEAL Team 10, kept them connected through comm equipment.

"Just remember, Fish, we're not here on vacation." Gator's gruff voice rattled in Jack's ear. Remy had been on SEAL Team 10 longer than Jack and had seen a lot more action. He'd taken Jack under his wing on his first day in the unit.

"It's hard to keep that in mind when the water's so clear I can see fifty feet down. I'd rather bust out my scuba gear and do some recreational diving." Jack adjusted his sunglasses. "You sure there's not some old abandoned shipwreck we can't blow up close by?"

"Save it for when we nail the pirates who've been stealing boats around here," Gator said. "No doubt we'll have plenty of action and opportunities to blow up shit."

Jack stared out at serene blue waters along the coastline of Honduras. As smooth and calm as the bay was, this area had seen its share of trouble. In the past month, four expensive pleasure yachts had been hijacked and disappeared. Their rich owners had been taken hostage by leftist guerillas operating under the name Castillo Commando. Most of the hostages had been ransomed and released, their ransom dollars used to fund the guerilla activities.

In the latest attack, they'd stolen a yacht owned by wealthy American business owner William Bentley and his nephew. His high-powered political contacts included the Secretary of Defense, who called in the Navy SEALs to locate and recover the missing hostages and eliminate the leftist guerrilla pirates from the Honduran coastline.

Jack, along with a twenty-two-man team from SEAL Team 10, had been deployed to handle the mission labeled Operation Constrictor.

They'd located the scuttled yachts in a nearby island inlet, but hadn't found the hideout of the Castillo Commando. Their only lead was a few satellite images of a couple of boats landing on the bay of Trujillo around midnight the day Bentley disappeared.

The Secretary of Defense, along with Bentley's wife, secured another yacht to use as a decoy loaded with Navy SEALs and complex intelligence-gathering equipment to help them recover the missing yacht owners and eradicate the guerrilla pirates. Four days had passed and no pirates had come or gone from the shores of the bay. They hadn't taken the bait or even come out to sniff around.

"Some vacation, huh?" Jack said as he strolled along the beach, collecting seashells.

"At least you're on the beach with half a chance of seeing women in bikinis," Swede grumbled.

"All we have here are some kids playing and old men in fishing boats." Jack stopped on the sand and performed a three-hundred-sixty-degree turn. In one direction were the old men and fishing boats. In the other was an empty skiff dragged up on the shore.

Jack lifted his hand to shade his eyes from the sun sinking lower over the jungle. At the edge of the sand in the shade of the jungle was a small gathering of dark-skinned locals. They seemed to be crowding around a group set up under a tent awning.

Curious, Jack set off across the sand to check it out, feeling a little naked without his combat gear or even a weapon as part of his attempt to appear as a bored, rich young man looking for something to do. Because he had the fewest tattoos of his SEAL brothers and he rocked a California surfer look that usually captured attention, he'd been chosen as the lure.

As he neared the gathering, he heard a voice call out in Spanish, "Please, wait your turn."

Standing at the edge of the gathering, Jack noted a woman holding a child with a skin rash over his belly. Another woman held a little girl with long black hair who cried softly against her mother's breast. A long jagged gash in her leg looked like it wasn't healing properly.

A narrow gap opened in the throng, giving Jack a view of the focus of the locals' attention. Three men and two women wearing scrubs sat on campstools with a folding table between them. One by one, they examined each patient, cleaning wounds, stitching lacerations and prescribing cleaning techniques. Some of the patients received shots, others pills, but they were all treated with a smile and gentle words and gestures.

A bald man in scrubs led a woman and a small child to a pretty medical worker with light brown hair and green eyes. She wore green scrubs and had her hair pulled back in a messy bun with tendrils falling around her cheeks.

"Dr. Rhoades," the man said in English. "This child needs your attention."

The woman smiled at the dark-eyed little girl who limped toward her followed by an older woman. When they got close, the child

4

buried her face in the old woman's skirt, crying.

The older woman spoke in rapid Spanish. "My granddaughter was bitten by a spider. Her leg is swollen and painful, and she is frightened of the doctor, afraid she will take her away from her family."

Smiling, the woman with the soft brown hair and gentle face rose from the campstool and dropped to her knees in the sand, putting herself on eye-level with the little girl. She spoke quietly in halting Spanish, smiling gently.

Jack couldn't hear her words, but he fell under her spell just as easily as the child.

The little girl nodded.

Dr. Rhoades spoke again.

The child and her grandmother both laughed.

When the doctor held out her hand, the little girl took it and allowed the doctor draw her onto her lap. She let the child listen to her own heartbeat through her stethoscope before she listened. Then she set the girl on the table beside her and examined her leg. By the time she'd cleaned and bandaged the leg, the little girl was smiling. Then she and her grandmother both hugged her and thanked her for helping them.

As Jack watched the line of locals slowly dissipate, he noticed the sun had slipped lower in the sky, making the shadows thicken on the edge of the trees. A shout caught his attention, drawing it away from the medical team.

Pushing his way through the remaining patients, a scrawny teenager spoke, waving his hands toward a dirt road. He grabbed a woman's arm and dragged her in the opposite direction. He let go and took another's hand and pulled her along, leading her away from the medical team and the dirt road that had him so upset. He turned back and ran toward the doctor, shouting hysterically.

Jack stiffened and glanced around, realizing he'd zoned out while watching Dr. Rhoades work with her patients. To keep the teen from reaching the doctor, Jack stepped in front of him.

The boy tried to dodge him.

Jack grabbed his arms.

The teen shouted something in Spanish but he was so distraught, Jack had a hard time understanding him. Two words stood out in the rest of his hysterical shouts. Castillo Commando.

Jack stiffened.

As if someone pulled the plug on a sink, the remaining locals disappeared into the trees.

Frantic, the boy twisted until he broke loose of Jack's hold and raced into the trees.

The doctor and the others wearing scrubs quickly packed their medical kits, folded tables and chairs and hurried toward the boat on the beach, glancing back over their shoulders.

"What's going on, Fish?" Gator spoke in his ear.

"Not sure, but I think the Commandos are coming." He stared at the shadowy woods, shocked not a single local could be seen. If he hadn't observed them for himself, he would have thought the beach had always been deserted.

The sound of gunfire from the dirt road at the far end of the beach jerked his attention to the north. A truck sped toward the medical personnel.

Jack bolted for the jet ski. His gaze shot to the doctor's small group.

One man dropped back to get behind the female doctor. No sooner had he let her go ahead of him, he jerked and grabbed his leg. He dropped the chair he'd been holding and limped as fast as he could, leaving a trail of blood in the sand. The rest of the crew ran across the sand to the little boat and threw in the chairs and tables. They turned and helped the injured man into the boat and then pushed off as, one by one, they jumped in, landing at odd angles.

The doctor and the bald guy were the last to climb aboard and the water was getting deep.

"Go! Go! Go!" The bald guy yelled as he pointed toward the open water.

SEAL's Obsession

Dr. Rhoades dragged herself over the side of the boat and fell into the bottom.

The tattooed bald man jumped in, and all of them ducked low as bullets pelted the water around them.

From a crouch, Jack shoved the jet ski across the sand and into the water, hitting the start button. The engine stuttered. "Start, dammit!" He hit the button again and the engine roared to life. Gunning the throttle, he rocketed out into the bay, laying low over the machine.

"What's going on, Fish?" Swede demanded.

"We're under attack. I'd say we found our guerillas." Jack swung wide to follow the little boat chugging toward a larger one, it's side marked with a big red cross, anchored in the bay. They'd almost reached it when a jet boat, equipped with a mounted machinegun and a dozen armed men rounded the spit at the edge of the bay, barreling toward the ship. The skiff filled with medical personnel barely slid alongside the bigger boat as the attackers opened fire.

"Shit!" Jack called out, feeling helpless and outgunned.

"A little intel would help, Jack," Swede prompted.

"A fully-armed gun boat is heading toward what I suspect is a floating medical boat in the bay here. I could use some air

8

support about now."

"Scrambling the Black Hawk. ETA ten mikes."

His body tensed. "There won't be anything left in ten minutes."

"Hold that thought." Swede went silent for a few precious seconds and came back on. "It's your lucky day. The Black Hawk is airborne. The fact they got restless is working in your favor. ETA five minutes. Think you can hold off the guerillas for that long?"

"Sure. No weapons and nothing but a jet ski?" Jack snorted. "I've got this."

"We have a boat on the way, ETA five mikes."

Jack kept heading for the medical boat. As he neared, he noted all hands were on deck to secure the skiff and get the bigger boat underway. Only one man stood on deck with a handgun. The weapon would be too little too late once the machine gun came within range.

He had to do something. Turning away from the big medical boat, he steered toward the fully-equipped gunboat. One unarmed man in nothing but swim trunks, riding a jet ski against a boatload of guerillas. The odds didn't look good, but when did a SEAL run from a challenge?

*The only easy day was yesterday.*

He aimed dead center of the bow, knowing the placement of the machinegun would be most effective off the port or starboard. As long as none of the guerillas moved forward with their rifles, Jack might get close enough to…

Hell if he knew. This wasn't one of those carefully crafted operations where the team practiced every move from start to finish in mockups of their target. This was ad-lib, and he was going it alone. No one had his six, or laid down supporting fire to keep the bad guys occupied long enough for him to close the distance.

As he neared the gunboat, he spotted three guerillas moving to the front, bringing their weapons to their shoulders.

*So much for the element of surprise.*

Jack zigzagged as he closed on the boat and dodged to the right, leaning hard to create a large rooster tail of a splash, drenching the armed men. Unfortunately, the turn placed him on the starboard side of the gunboat, giving the machine gunner a perfect target.

Bullets pelted the water all around him as he zigzagged across the ocean's surface. One clipped his thigh, tearing through his favorite swim trunks. *Well, damn.*

"Come on, air support!" he yelled, throttle wide open as he led the gunboat away from the craft the doctor and her staff had boarded and set underway.

With the roar of the jet ski in his ears, he didn't hear the Black Hawk until he saw it swoop in and strafe the gunboat with fifty-caliber bullets.

Dr. Natalie Rhoades hovered on the deck of the *Nightingale*, watching as the man on the jet ski headed straight for the guerilla gunship, her heart lodged in her throat. "Is that guy insane?"

"He's buying us time to get away," Mac Pennington, a bald, tattooed combat medic, stood at her side, shaking his head. "And yes, he's insane."

The drumbeat of helicopter rotors filled the air as a Black Hawk helicopter popped over the shoreline trees and headed straight for the gunboat.

Hallie Kristofer joined Natalie and Mac, clapping her hands. "Yay! The cavalry has arrived!"

The machine gunners abandoned their attack on the man on the jet ski and focused on the helicopter.

With the Black Hawk keeping the gunboat full of leftist guerillas engaged, the jet ski turned toward their boat. They had barely gotten underway when he caught up to them.

"We have a visitor, Skipper!" Mac shouted.

"Should we stop?" Hallie asked.

Natalie gripped the rail. "Yes, of course. He saved us from the guerillas, the least we can do is bring him on board and thank him properly."

"Steve and the Skipper are the only ones with guns on the boat." Mac stretched to look overboard toward the rider. "Skipper has to drive the boat, and with Steve out of commission due to the gunshot wound, should I get his gun?"

"No, I saw this man on the shore," Natalie said. "He looked pretty harmless." She was stretching it by saying he looked harmless. Unarmed would have been a better description. The man was big, like he worked out...a lot. He didn't have a spare ounce of flesh on his body and the tattoos on his shoulders and back gave him a motorcycle rider, bad-boy appearance. But those clear blue eyes and shaggy blond hair softened that image. He could have been any beach bum off the coast of California. Either way, he'd made more of an impression on her than she cared to admit.

"Looks can be deceiving," Hallie warned with a frown.

Natalie nodded. "But he risked his life and saved us from attack. We have to give him the benefit of a doubt."

"I'll go help Daphne and Jean-David," Mac said. "Just to be sure."

"I'm coming, too," Natalie said. "We'll go under the assumption that there is safety in numbers."

A shout rose up from the back of the

boat, "Throw me a line!"

The boat slowed. Ship's deckhand, Daphne Bradford, tossed the man a line off the back.

He grabbed it and dragged himself and the jet ski up to tie onto the dinghy at the rear. Jean-David and Mac both held out their hands to help him on board.

The jet ski rider grabbed one of each and let them haul him onboard.

Hallie turned and shouted toward the pilot house, "Go!"

The engine engaged and the *Nightingale* sped away from the gunboat that was still taking fire from the Black Hawk.

Natalie stepped forward, her pulse kicking up as she faced the man with all the muscles. Up close, he was much larger than when he'd been standing on the edge of the crowd of women and children on shore.

"Who's in charge?" he asked, scanning the three on deck.

Her knees wobbling more than they should have, Natalie stepped forward. "I am. Welcome aboard the *Nightingale*. Thank you for saving us from the guerillas." She held out her hand.

He took it in his, those blue eyes shining as she gave it a firm shake.

"I'm Jack Fischer. Thanks for letting me come on board. My jet ski was getting low on fuel. I wasn't sure I'd make it back to my boat.

How's the guy who got shot?"

Hallie answered before Natalie could. "Dr. Biacowski is working with him now."

Natalie had taken a cursory look at the wound. "He should be okay, barring any infection." She glanced around the end of the bay. "What boat did you say you came from?"

"I'm with some buddies of mine on the *Pegasus.*" Jack pointed to a large pleasure yacht anchored near the southern end of the large bay.

Even from a distance, Natalie could see the gleaming white hull of the craft. She glanced back at Jack. He didn't quite fit the image she had of a rich yacht owner on vacation.

His lips quirked and he stared down at his naked torso with the tattoos and his torn shorts. "I'm working for my passage aboard the yacht."

Blood dripped off the bottom hem of Jack's black swim trunks onto the white deck.

"You're bleeding!" Hallie hooked his arm and led him toward a bench. "Come over here and sit down. Mac, could you get Dr. Rhoades's bag?"

"It's right here. I've got it." Natalie grabbed her satchel from where it landed when they transferred from the dinghy. She'd been content to stand back and let Hallie and Mac do all the talking, but with an injury at hand, her natural instinct was to heal.

Hallie pushed Jack onto a bench. "If you'll hand me the scissors, I'll cut away the fabric."

Natalie pulled her surgical scissors from the bag. "No need. I can do this," she told her nurse.

Hallie moved away, giving Natalie room to kneel in front of Jack. When she raised her scissors to cut away the fabric, Jack jerked his leg out of range.

"I happen to like these swim trunks. If it's all the same to you, I can pull them up." A grin spread across his face. "Unless you want me to take them off."

Natalie's eyes widened and her breath caught in her throat. He was practically naked already and she was breathless. She was afraid she'd pass out if he were completely nude. Mentally chastising herself, she focused on the injury, not the man. Hell, she'd seen naked women, children and men. Jack Fischer was no different. Every body had much the same characteristics.

Jack just had more in all the right places.

Heat rose up her neck and suffused her cheeks at that errant thought. "Just pull it up," she said, her voice squeaking, causing the heat in her cheeks to intensify.

"Wow," Hallie said. "You've got some powerful thighs."

"Hallie!" Dr. Rhoades snapped, not so much because of the inappropriateness of her statement, but because she'd been thinking it herself. "Put your tongue back in your head and hand me some gauze and alcohol."

Hallie winked at Jack. "Your shoulders are anatomically exceptional, as well." She opened the bottle of alcohol and handed it and the gauze to Natalie. "Is that better?" she asked, batting her eyelashes.

Mac snorted. "Seriously, Hallie?"

Natalie tipped the bottle of alcohol over the gauze. "He's a patient, not an entertainer at a strip club."

Jack's sudden bark of laughter startled Natalie and she spilled alcohol onto his leg, some of which found its way into his wound. His laughter turned into a slight hiss. "God, that feels good," he said through gritted teeth.

"Good Lord," Hallie muttered. "He even makes pain look sexy."

"He's just a guy. A beach bum," Mac noted.

"I'm employed," Jack corrected, his eyes gleaming with mischief. "I gave up being a bum for a paycheck and a chance to see the world, one exotic port at a time."

Natalie couldn't help but get caught up in Jack's rich, deep tone and playful expression. Pushing back her shoulders, she applied the soaked gauze to his wound.

This time he didn't flinch, his gaze on hers as she held the gauze with a firm touch, gauging his tolerance for pain. Then she cleaned the area and held out her hand. "Dry gauze, please."

Hallie handed Natalie more gauze. "Sounds romantic." She sighed. "So, Jack, do you have a girl in every port?"

"Hallie!" Natalie clapped the gauze over the injury a little harder than she would have liked.

Jack smiled, his jaw tight. "Are you this gentle with all your patients, Dr. Rhoades?"

"Ignore Hallie," Mac said with a shake of his head. "She's been cooped up on the boat too long. I think she needs a night out."

Hallie crossed her arms over her chest, her chin lifting in challenge. "You're right. I could use a night out." Her mouth curled into a saucy grin. "But it would be so much better if the night was with Jack."

Mac's jaw tightened. "I see." He turned toward Natalie. "Do you need me for anything, Dr. Rhoades?"

She glanced at his taut face and almost asked him what was wrong, but Mac looked like he could bite the cap off a bottle of beer with his teeth. "No, thank you. Perhaps Dr. Biacowski could use your skills with Steve. I'm worried he hasn't come up from below."

"I'll check." Mac turned on his heels and stalked away.

Natalie waited until Mac had disappeared below deck until she said, "Hallie, I'd like for you to go, too."

"But you don't have anyone here to assist you."

"I can manage Mr. Fischer's wound care on my own now, thank you."

"What if he's working with the guerillas and attacks you?"

Natalie glanced up into eyes a beautiful shade of blue and she gulped. "Mr. Fischer, are you going to attack me?"

He hesitated, his eyes flaring. Then he shook his head. "Not unless you want me to."

Hallie choked on her laughter. "I knew he was a bad boy. He has it written all over him."

"Hallie," Natalie warned, though, at times, she wished she could be as direct as Hallie. The younger woman had nailed it—the man had bad boy written all over every inch of his incredible body.

"What?" Hallie raised her hands. "I can't help that I worry about you."

"Daphne and Jean-David are on deck. If I need assistance, I can call out to them." Natalie tipped her head toward the door.

"I'm going." Hallie's lips firmed into a tight line. "Though the view is much better out here than in the cabin." She left, glancing over her shoulder one last time before she disappeared through the cabin door.

Tearing adhesive tape from a roll, Natalie secured the gauze to Jack's thick, tanned thigh, her fingers pressing into the solid muscle. She pressed the adhesive several times to be sure it stuck—not that she was gauging the hardness of his muscle. He smelled of sun and salt water, and his shoulders were so broad they blocked the light from the setting sun from glaring into her eyes.

"Nice work, doc." He stood and pulled her to her feet.

She stood so close, she felt the heat radiating off his body and had to fight the urge to touch him.

The boat rocked in the waves and she fell against that hard, muscular chest, her palms planting against the smooth, taut plains.

His arm came up around her waist, clamping her against him, her hips firmly pressed against his. "I've got you," he assured her.

His soothing tones did nothing to slow her racing pulse. Boy did he, with strong arms and a rock-solid body. Natalie's body lit up like a furnace.

"So, what's the prognosis, doc?"

His lips were so close she could feel the warmth of his breath. "Prognosis?" she whispered. All coherent thought escaped her as she curled her fingers into his skin.

"Will I live?" he asked.

"I don't know." She shifted her gaze up to his eyes and fell into the deep blue orbs. "It's too soon to tell."

"Perhaps this will help you decide." He

bent to brush his lips lightly over hers.

Normally one to hold every man at arm's length, Natalie didn't protest. She was powerless to resist as his kiss grew more insistent and he claimed her mouth.

When he allowed her up for air, she stared into his eyes.

The boat shifted again and her bag slid across the deck, bumping into the backs of her ankles, returning her to her senses. "Let go of me."

Jack's eyes narrowed, his brows drawing together. "My apologies for being so forward." He dropped his arm from around her waist and stepped back.

Natalie immediately missed the warmth of his embrace, but she couldn't let him kiss her again. She had a strict personal code of not fooling around with the crewmembers.

A tiny voice in her head reminded her he wasn't a member of *her* crew.

Either way, she wasn't interested in getting involved with any man. She'd already had one good marriage with a man she loved. She doubted seriously she could be so fortunate as to find another man who could rise to that level. "I'll have Skipper bring you close enough to your boat to get there by jet ski. I think it best if you leave, now."

# Chapter Two

Jack stood on the deck as they neared the luxury yacht, the *Pegasus*. Dr. Rhoades had disappeared into the boat's cabin, leaving him alone. The man and woman he'd seen working the deck had disappeared, too.

He scanned the bay, looking for the gunboat. After the Black Hawk had come to call, the gunboat disappeared around the curve of the coastline. The Black Hawk eventually returned to its temporary landing zone to wait for another call to action.

"Status, Fish?" Swede spoke in his ear.

Jack shot a quick look around to be certain he was alone. "Did the crew of the Black Hawk follow the gunboat back to its docking position?"

"They pulled up a narrow river and disappeared into the jungle. We're arranging for a boat drop into the area for tomorrow. Where are you?"

"I'm aboard the *Nightingale.*"

"The what?"

"*Nightingale*. A floating doctor boat. Its crew members are medical personnel who visit poor countries and provide free health care to the natives."

"When are you coming home?"

"Heading your way." Dr. Rhoades had given him his marching orders.

"What happened on the beach?"

His muscles tensed at the memory. "The guerillas chased the doctor and her staff off the beach and had a boat waiting in the bay to cut them off."

"You think they were trying to hijack the boat?"

"I'm not sure."

"We were in the same bay and the gunboat didn't even attempt to come after us."

"Could it be because our boat is filled with an overdose of testosterone? This medical boat could be had with little resistance. Only the skipper and one of the other crewmembers carry a gun."

"Are you kidding me?" Swede exclaimed.

"That's it. From what I can tell, the group's about fifty-fifty male to female."

"Lucky bastard. I'd like to see some females."

Jack wasn't complaining. Dr. Rhoades's dark eyes flashed in his memory. "I'm leaving as soon as the skipper brings this tub to a halt."

As he spoke, the floating doctor boat slowed and eased to a stop.

Jack strode to the back of the boat and pulled the line he'd used to tie off the jet ski, bringing it close enough so that he could climb aboard.

"Mr. Fischer," a gravelly female voice called out behind him.

He turned to face a tall, masculine woman with short, spiked silver hair. She hadn't been part of the boat's welcoming committee.

She stuck out her hand. "Ronnie Moore. I'm the skipper of the *Nightingale*."

"Nice to meet you, ma'am." He took her hand, amazed at how firm and strong her grip was.

"I saw what you did earlier to keep the guerillas off our tails while we got our boat underway." She gave him a single nod. "Thank you."

"You're welcome." He turned to go.

"Mr. Fischer, the purpose of this boat is to provide medical assistance to people who can't afford it or don't have access to decent care. We help with medicine, education and wound care. However, we can't help others if we're under attack. We could use someone like you to prevent future attacks."

Jack frowned. "What are you saying?"

"I have a gun and I know how to use it, but being out on the deck firing, when I need to be getting the *Nightingale* out of hostile situations, doesn't do much good." She scrubbed a hand over her spiky hair. "What I'm trying to say is that if you want a job doing some good for people, you've got it.

The pay sucks, but the food's good, when we can get fresh meat and produce."

"You're offering me a job?" He was so taken aback his shock must have shown on his face.

"We can't compete with the accommodations of a luxury yacht, but you'll have a hard time finding a more dedicated group of people who care."

"What does Dr. Rhoades think about me working on board the *Nightingale*?"

Ronnie's brows rose. "She's the one who suggested it. I drive the ship, but she runs the show."

Jack couldn't believe what he was hearing. The good doctor suggested he come to work for her crew? "I thought she wanted me to leave."

The skipper shrugged. "She saw reason and changed her mind."

This was a switch in direction Jack hadn't seen coming. "Wow, I don't know."

"Think about it. Dr. Rhoades is a good doctor and an even better person. Not a soul on this boat wouldn't give his life for her, and she's saved so many. You'd be expected to fill in wherever is needed, but mostly, we need someone to provide protection for the staff, especially the doctors. They're a scarce commodity down here and are often targets of kidnappings."

He could see it. In the poorest of villages,

a doctor was even scarcer than food. "I'll consider it and let you know."

Ronnie stuck out her hand. "I'm sure you'll make the right decision. What you did today was very brave and ballsy."

"Thanks." He let go of the skipper's hand and climbed onto the jet ski, hit the start switch and tossed the line back onto the *Nightingale*. As he backed away, he glanced at the boat filled with medical staff who gave of their time and services not for financial gain, but because doing so was the right thing. And after seeing Dr. Rhoades with the little girl earlier, he could tell providing healthcare was something she was very good at and that her heart was in her work and the welfare of her patients.

As he pushed the throttle lever, he caught a glimpse of soft brown hair that had escaped its messy bun and was lifted by the sea breeze. Dr. Natalie Rhoades stood on the deck, her gaze following him as he sped across the water toward the *Pegasus*.

Gator, Irish and Dustman stood on the deck, watching him as he closed the distance between him and the borrowed yacht. Gator and Dustman wore dark swim trunks similar to the ones they trained in back at Little Creek. Irish, in keeping with the playboy image of a rich young man on a yacht, wore a bright red, butt-hugging suit, which barely contained his junk. They waved like vacationing rich guys, greeting one of their own returning from a shore jaunt.

Jack drove the jet ski up onto the loading platform specially designed to quick-park the rich man's toys and climbed off.

"Well?" Irish met him at the rear of the boat. "Did you get close enough to the gunboat to make out any faces on board?"

Jack shook his head. "I was too busy dodging bullets." He rubbed the wound on his leg. It twinged when he walked, but was nothing compared to others he'd received in battle.

Dustman joined them. "What? You didn't hop on board and go all John Wayne?"

With a snort, Jack pushed past Irish and Dustman. "Not today. Maybe when I have someone covering my six. Where're Gator and Swede?"

Irish tipped his head toward the cabin. "Inside, waiting on you."

Jack hurried through sliding glass doors, a plan forming in his head.

The team had transformed the elaborate living area into a tactical operation center with computers lining one wall, tapping into the big television screens to display satellite and drone images. Swede sat at a granite bar, his weapon of choice—his laptop computer—open and displaying images of what had happened that day. "Do you see that? They weren't shooting at the female wearing the stethoscope around her neck, only the tall man." Swede hit a button on his keyboard and the video fast-forwarded to the bay chase where the gunners on the gunboat hadn't been firing at the little dinghy carrying the medical personnel. "They were trying to cut them off from making it to their boat."

"They didn't start firing at anything in particular until Fish got in their way and gave them a face full of saltwater." Gator leaned back and glanced over at Jack. "We got lucky. The drone was over the beach when it all went down. Swede captured the entire scene from a bird's eye view."

"I was there, I know what happened," Jack said.

Swede reset the video feed and played it again.

Jack leaned in to watch the footage. He pointed at the screen where the pretty, dark-haired woman grabbed her medical bag and a folding chair and ran for the boat. "That's Dr. Rhoades. She's in charge of the floating doctor boat." She was the last of the medical staff to head for the boat. The tall lanky guy saw she was behind him, so he stopped and urged her to go in front so he was covering her from behind. As they ran for the boat, he took a hit in the leg, dropped the chair he'd been carrying and limped the rest of the way. That had to be the man Dr. Rhoades had referred to as Steve. The others helped him into the boat, and Dr. Rhoades and Mac were the last to climb aboard.

"Who's the pretty blonde?" Irish asked.

"Hallie. I believe she's a nurse." Jack pointed at the bald man. "Hallie and Mac performed triage on the locals waiting in line."

Gator turned and paced across the spacious and tastefully decorated living area, his arms crossed. "The leftists haven't made a move on this yacht since we've been here and we've more or less been sitting ducks. They could have had us several times over."

"I didn't mind the first couple days because I'm working on my tan." Irish patted the array of freckles on his pale chest. The man never tanned worth shit. "But I'm ready for some action."

"Yeah, and Fish here goes on a joy ride and runs right into some." Dustman shook his head. "And he found the women, and I'm assuming, the only Americans within a hundred miles."

Gator paced back to the computer where Swede had started the video all over again. "They weren't interested in our bait. They seemed dead set on targeting the doctor's crew. Otherwise, they wouldn't have set up both a land and sea assault."

"Why?" Dustman asked. "I bet they don't have a ton of money. They probably operate off of donations."

"I guarantee they don't have a lot," Jack

confirmed. "The boat appeared to be well-maintained, but vintage. The group isn't heavily armed. From what they said, they only have two handguns on board."

Shaking his head, Irish gave a low whistle. "Are they just asking for trouble?"

"No, they're on a mission to help people, not shoot them."

"But anyone with any touch with reality would know these waters aren't safe."

"They get it now." Jack pushed a hand through his shaggy hair. "Look, if the expensive yacht isn't drawing out the pirates, we need to focus on what is."

Gator's brows narrowed. "You think we should use the doctor boat as bait?"

"I don't think we should use anyone on that boat as bait. But apparently, the Castillo Commandos could be interested in them. The point is, they aren't safe."

"And we haven't caught our pirates," Gator concluded. "You know the big boys at the top won't fund our little vacation indefinitely."

"Right. We need to position ourselves where we can do the most good and hope to catch at least one of the guerillas to lead us to the rest." Jack took a deep breath and jumped in. "The doctor and the skipper offered me a job on board the *Nightingale* to provide security."

Irish laughed out loud. "Did you tell

them that you already have a job?"

"I told them I was a deckhand on this yacht." He shrugged. "They want me to jump ship and go to work for them."

"They have money to lure you away from a cushy job?" Gator asked. "Maybe we underestimated the value of the crew. Perhaps one of them is the daughter of a rich oil magnate."

Jack smiled. "No, actually, I was told the group couldn't offer much. The skipper stated none of them worked for financial gain, but because it was the right thing to do."

Irish snorted. "In other words, you'd be working for peanuts."

An image of the little girl with the injured leg, and how grateful she and her grandmother had been to get any kind of medical assistance, flashed through Jack's mind. Payment wasn't always monetary.

"Cut to the chase, Fish. What are you proposing?" Gator asked.

"I think the doctor and her medical staff are targets of the guerilla group. We should put at least one of us on board, equipped with communication equipment to keep in touch and report back. These people go ashore where needed to provide medical assistance to the poor. When they are on shore, I could be part of the team as boots on the ground to provide security and intel should they be targeted again."

Gator's eyes narrowed, as if he was considering the proposal. "And you think having an inside guy would help?"

"Someone on board the *Nightingale* could provide the locations of their next stops," Jack said.

"I volunteer," Irish said, his gaze tracking an image on the screen. "That blonde is just what this frogman needs to keep him hopping."

Gator shook his head. "Sorry, Irish. Fish was offered the job."

"Damn," Irish swore. "I'd give my left nut to go with you."

"Save your nuts for the fight," Fish said with a wide grin.

Gator faced Jack. "Okay. Accept the lady doctor's offer."

His stomach fluttered and his pulse quickened at the thought of seeing the pretty doctor again. "I'll need some communication equipment that won't be too easily detected."

Swede dropped off the bar stool and strode across the floor to the hardened case full of everything they could possibly need for a surveillance and tactical operation.

"I'll get my duffle." Jack hurried to the beautifully designed stateroom he'd been assigned to share with Dustin "Dustman" Ford. Each man had a twin bed tucked against opposite walls. Drawers, closets and cubbies provided more storage than the studio apartment he had back in Virginia.

He pulled his duffle out of the closet, jammed shorts, polo shirts, T-shirts and undergarments into the bag along with his shaving kit and tennis shoes. As for weapons, he couldn't really go on board the Nightingale fully loaded with all he'd brought on this mission. He tucked his nine-millimeter pistol in with his underwear and added the little H&K 40-caliber pistol he could fit practically anywhere. That left his rifles. Most were too long to stash in his duffle. But he had one that could break down into separate pieces for storage and ease of packing into small places. The weapon was lightweight and quick to assemble with a one-hundred meter range. He doubted the skipper or Steve's weapons would have near the power or accuracy of any of his.

At the last minute, he folded in the dress slacks and shoes he'd been ordered to bring in case they needed to stage a fancy dinner party on the *Pegasus,* or if they needed to establish themselves as rich visitors with the local authorities. A ruse to make themselves known to the guerillas.

With all the clothes and weapons he needed packed into his duffle, he went back to the living area where Swede had another bag lined with a towel and filled with electronics.

"I can't take all that. I'm likely to share a

room with someone else. Stashing that much stuff would be hard." He picked through the bag. "I need comm in my ear, several GPS tracking devices and a handheld tracker."

"What about weapons?"

"I have two pistols and my breakdown rifle."

"Here, take some explosives, detonators and grenades." Dustman jammed them into the side pouches of his duffle bag. "You never know when you'll need them."

Laden down with more than he thought he could get away with, Jack headed for the back of the yacht and the jet ski.

Gator followed, detailing a communication protocol as to when he should check in and how often.

Jack nodded, stuck the communication device that looked like a hearing aid into his ear and climbed aboard the jet ski. "Let's catch us some pirates."

Natalie paced the length of the *Nightingale's* dining area. "We can't operate in a hostile environment."

Her team had gathered—some seated at the table, others leaning against the wall, out of her way while she paced.

"We signed on knowing the dangers of working in Honduras," Mac said. "The situation's not nearly as bad as what I dealt with in Afghanistan."

Natalie shot him a frown. "True, but we're not in Afghanistan, and not all of us are Army-trained combat medics. We don't have the tactical experience to fight off an enemy attack."

"We should call it and move farther north," Steve said. "Back to Costa Rica. That area isn't having nearly the issues with guerillas, and I'm sure a lot of people there need our help as much."

"We just worked our way through the shores of Costa Rica. The people of Honduras are in bad shape. Not only have they been dealing with a corrupt government, but they have to endure the guerillas injuring innocents." Natalie shook her head. "I can't abandon them. Some of these people are in desperate need."

"And we will be no good to them if we're dead." Steve rubbed his injured leg.

Natalie stared at his hand, smoothing over the gunshot wound he'd received courtesy of the guerillas. "You're right, Steve. I can't expect any of you to risk going into an area as volatile as Honduras. Asking that is not fair of me."

"Who's asking? We're volunteering." Hallie lifted her hand. "All those who are okay with continuing our mission as originally planned, raise your hand."

Every member of the medical staff raised his or her hand, except Steve. He glanced around at the others. "We're making a big mistake," he warned as he slowly raised his hand.

"We're in," Mac stated. "Now, can we call it a night? I want to double-check our medical supplies and repack our shore kits for tomorrow."

"I'll help," Natalie insisted. "The rest of you get some rest. Today's been busy and tomorrow will involve even more work."

"Hopefully without the added excitement of a guerilla attack," Dr. Biacowski said. "You should stay on the boat tomorrow and let me do shore duty."

Natalie stared at the older doctor. His face was still pale and he was still weak from his bout with dysentery from something he ate at one of their stops. "Today was hard on your body, Craig. Until you're back at one hundred percent, I want you to stay on the *Nightingale*."

"I tell you, I'm feeling much better. A good night's sleep and I'll be ready to go," he argued.

Crossing her arms over her chest, she gave him a pointed look. "Yeah, and if we have another day like today and have to run like the wind, could you keep up?"

The man started to open his mouth, then sighed and shook his head. "Probably not."

"End of discussion," Natalie said, brooking no argument. "You're to stay on the boat. We need someone back here to take care of us if anything should go wrong, like it did today."

Hallie patted the doctor's face. "Don't worry, there will be more sick people for you to heal when you get better. You need to stay in as much as possible and get better in a hurry. After we set up the clinic on the beach tomorrow, we're supposed to sail over to the port at Trujillo. Their annual patron saint festival is in two nights. We're all due a little R&R."

"Is it safe to go to the festival, after what happened today?" Steve pushed to his feet, balancing all his weight on his uninjured leg.

"The town should be okay. Enough people are there, between the locals and tourists. And the Honduran military will have an increased presence for the event. I checked. We should be okay," Hallie said. "Dr. Rhoades will go, won't you?"

"I don't know." After the attack that day, Natalie wasn't sure about anything.

"You have to go. The trip wouldn't be the same without you. Besides, some of the locals asked you to be there. And I'm sure the ones we see when we set up the clinic in Trujillo will be as eager to see you there, as well."

She did try to make an effort to join festivities put on by the locals. They were more open if she and the crew participated in important events. "I'll go with you. I could use a little relaxation, especially after today."

"Me, too," Hallie said. "I'm ready to get off the boat for a little wine and dancing." She grabbed Mac's hand and spun beneath his arm. "What do you say? Will you dance with me?"

Mac's mouth tightened. "I'm not much of a dancer."

Hallie propped her fists on her hips. "Steve, are you going?"

Steve shook his head.

"Exactly. Jean-David will probably stay with the boat. Dr. Biacowski, do you dance?"

"I gave up my dancing shoes in my undergrad days." He patted his stomach, appearing glad to use his ailment as an excuse. "I'd rather stay aboard the boat and read a good book. I don't want to risk being out of commission for any more time than I already have."

Hallie turned to Mac. "That leaves you." She put both hands together under her chin and batted her eyelashes. "Please?"

"Okay, fine." He stepped around her. "That is, *if* we go and *if* there isn't any trouble in town. Now, if you'll excuse me, I'm preparing for tomorrow's village visit."

"I'm coming with you." Natalie followed him out of the dining area to hit the storeroom where they kept all the equipment and medication locked up in case the boat was in dock and someone tried to come aboard. She used her key to open the door and led the way inside.

"I heard Skipper talking to that jet ski rider," Mac said.

"Jack?" Natalie corrected. She knew where Mac was headed before he opened his mouth, so she beat him to the punch. "I asked her to offer him a position on board the *Nightingale*."

"That's what I heard. I was hoping the offer was a mistake."

"We need protection."

"What can one guy do against an army of guerillas?"

Natalie turned to face him. "You were there. You saw what he could do. He distracted them long enough for us to get a head start."

"If not for the Black Hawk helicopter, he would have been killed. We don't need a martyr who likes to hotdog on a jet ski." His lips formed a tight line. "And where the hell did that Black Hawk come from?"

"Skipper said she'd heard from one of the other ships in the area that a U.S. Army Black Hawk helicopter unit was staging a training exercise somewhere around here. She thinks it's to establish a presence because of the increased guerilla activity." Natalie pulled a bottle of amoxicillin from a shelf and checked the expiration date before placing it into the case they carried into the field. She added several vials of prophylaxes for malaria, measles, mumps, and rubella to those already in the case. As many children as they could vaccinate, the better.

"Steve had a very good point." Mac took the vials from her hands and placed them carefully in the elastic bands specially attached to the inside of the case to keep them from banging around in transport. "Today was too close. We could have been killed."

"We've already gone over this." She checked the case, mentally ticking off what they would need for the next day's sick call clinic. "If you don't feel comfortable going ashore, stay on board."

"And leave you without any protection?" Mac shook his head. "Not a chance."

"We'll be sure to watch for trouble and stay close enough to the skiff to make a quick getaway."

"There will only be three of us tomorrow."

She knew he was right, but she couldn't disappoint the locals. "We already put out the word that we'd be there. Those children need medical care."

Mac checked one more time, before closing the medical kit. When he straightened, he caught Natalie's arm. "I know how much you care about these people. But you need to think about yourself sometimes."

Her heart squeezed so tightly in her chest it hurt. "Mac, I have to do this."

"Why?"

She stared up at him and, for a moment, thought about telling him her life story. But she didn't want to burden him with her heartache. This project was her dream, a dream born of tragedy. Mac, of all of them, would understand. He'd watched members of his unit die, even had some of them die in his arms.

"I just have to." She ducked around him and headed for the outside deck. When the memories surfaced, they rose up like a volcano shooting out the top of a mountain— fast, hot and furious. She fought them back, refusing to sink into that black abyss of depression that hovered on the edge of her psyche.

Jean-David had the helm for the first half of the night, and Daphne would take over the last half. Ronnie had taken them out to one of the nearby islands and anchored off the coast, away from the mainland. They would head back in the next day to set up their makeshift clinic at one of the villages. Then they'd move on to Trujillo and spend the night anchored close to the town.

Alone on the deck, Natalie gave in to the rush of emotions that had been building throughout the day. Tomorrow would have been her daughter's fifth birthday. Emma

40

hadn't lived to see her first. She'd been only eight months old when they'd been sideswiped by an eighteen-wheeler whose driver had fallen asleep. Their car had gone off the road and rolled over and over down a steep embankment and then burst into flame.

Natalie had been thrown from the vehicle and knocked unconscious. Her husband, Andrew, and baby Emma hadn't been as fortunate. Their seatbelts had held secure all the way to the bottom of the hill when the vehicle was engulfed in fire.

The smell of smoke still had the power to make her choke on her memories. She'd come to when the car exploded, shaking the ground beneath her. She'd stayed conscious only long enough to permanently imprint the fiery inferno on her memory.

Standing on the deck of the *Nightingale*, she inhaled deep breaths, sucking in the salty, tangy air of the tropics. Struggling to push thoughts of Emma and Andrew to the back of her mind. After almost five years, she thought the pain would have dulled. She'd left Colorado, left the mountains and the place where she'd grown up to escape the memories. Nothing about the sea reminded her of Andrew and Emma. Never again could she live in the mountains. They closed in around her, making her remember too much, reminding her of all she'd lost that night.

Little Emma, the happiest baby, with

chubby cheeks and a smile that would melt her heart every time, had just been learning to walk. She could say dada, mama and bye-bye. One moment, they were a happy little family of three, and in the blink of an eye, Natalie was alone.

A tear slipped from the corner of her eye.

Natalie clenched her fist, willing herself to stop. But another tear followed the first and before long, a steady stream trailed down her cheeks. The ship's generator drowned out all other sounds and hopefully, the sobs she couldn't manage to contain. She stood in the moonlight, letting her tears flow unchecked. Get it out, she told herself. Push out the pain and move on with life. She was alive for a reason and that reason was to help others. Otherwise, she might as well have died in the crash that killed Andrew and Emma.

"Dr. Rhoades," a deep voice said behind her.

Natalie sucked in a sob and held her breath, unable to turn or answer.

"Natalie?"

The deep rich tone wrapped around her, filling the cold, lonely place she'd let herself slide into. Big, capable hands curled around her arms and turned her to face him.

Jack Fischer stood before her, his blue eyes reflecting the moonlight, his brows furrowed. "Are you all right?" he asked.

She opened her mouth to tell him that

she was, but nothing came out. Instead, more tears flowed down her cheeks.

In a flash, he pulled her into his arms and held her close. "Tell me what's wrong. Maybe I can help."

She leaned her cheek against his chest, absorbing his warmth and strength. "No one can," she whispered past the lump in her throat. "They're gone forever."

# Chapter Three

When Jack had arrived back at the *Nightingale*, Jean-David greeted him and threw him a line. Once on board, the deckhand told him the medical staff was having a meeting in the dining hall in the cabin. By the time he'd found his way to the dining area, the meeting had broken up. Hallie had been there, making a cup of tea. When she saw him, she immediately hugged him and said something about having another dance partner at the festival.

Jack wasn't sure what that was about. He just wanted to meet with Dr. Rhoades and let her know he would be coming to work on the *Nightingale* as head of security.

Hallie told him he might find Dr. Rhoades in the storeroom or her stateroom. The storeroom turned out to be locked, and she hadn't answered his knock on her stateroom door.

Finally, he went up on deck, thinking she might be having a final chat with the skipper before they called it a night. He found her, not in the pilothouse but on the forward deck, her shoulders slumped and shaking.

Not wanting to intrude, he stopped and listened for a moment. At the sound of a

Elle James

muffled sob, he'd moved forward, calling out her name.

Now he stood with her wrapped in his arms. The take-charge doctor, melting with emotion. He gave her a moment or two, but when his shirt grew damp, he couldn't take it any longer. As a SEAL, he preferred to charge in and slay the demons. He was a fixer, not a nurturer.

"Hey, that was my favorite shirt." Jack captured her face in both hands and turned it up to his. Moonlight glistened off her wet cheeks and made the teardrops caught in her eyelashes sparkle. Even with a wet face and red-rimmed eyes, she was beautiful.

"I'm sorry," she said. "I got your shirt wet. I don't normally do this."

"I really don't care about the shirt. And if you need a shoulder to cry on, have at it. But tell me why and maybe I can help."

She shook her head. "Doesn't matter." Her bottom lip trembled, and a huge teardrop slipped from the corner of her eye and rolled down her cheek.

"Apparently, it does." With his thumb, he wiped away the tear.

"You shouldn't see me this way."

"Why? Because someone might see this as a sign of weakness and take advantage of the beautiful Dr. Rhoades?" Before he could think his action through logically, he brushed his lips across her forehead.

45

The doctor blinked up at him, her eyes wide. "Why did you do that?"

He shrugged. "I don't know. You looked like you need it." And he did it again. "Someone needed to kiss your booboo and I'm not certain where it is. Rather than offend you, I chose the forehead. It's the least controversial place I could kiss and not get slapped for doing so." He raised his eyebrows in challenge. "You're not going to slap me, are you?"

She caught the trembling lip with her pearly white teeth and shook her head. "No. But you probably shouldn't do that again."

"You're right. It wouldn't be right for me to kiss you when you're my new boss."

"What?" She leaned back and frowned.

He dropped his hands from her face and captured her around the waist to steady her on the deck. "You heard right. I've decided to take you up on your offer to work for the *Nightingale*. If you still want me." His fingers tightened on her waist. "Do you still want me?"

"I don't know." She stared up into his eyes, the tears having dried in her own. "You'd have to promise not to kiss me again."

Jack shook his head. "I can't do that."

"Why?"

"What if you *want* me to kiss you? I'd have to break my promise."

"I won't," she said, her gaze shifting to

his lips,

An action that belied her words. Hope crept into his thoughts. "Are you sure?"

She sighed and leaned against him. "I'm not sure of anything, anymore." For a moment, she remained pressed against his chest, then she pushed away and stepped out of his reach. Dr. Rhoades held out her hand. "Welcome aboard as the newest member of the *Nightingale* floating doctor boat."

He took her hand and shook it when he'd much rather pull her back into his arms and hold her there until she told him what made her cry. "Thank you."

"I'll show you where you can stow your gear. You'll have to bunk with Mac. We're very limited on space, so I can't give you a separate room."

"I'm used to bunking with others. Even as a deckhand aboard a yacht, I had to share a room with another guy."

"Well, good." She started to go around him.

He caught her hand. "Why were you crying, Natalie?" he asked softly.

She stared at his hand holding hers and didn't answer at first.

After a full minute, he was about to let go when she spoke.

"Tomorrow would have been my Emma's fifth birthday." Then she pulled her hand free and hurried by.

*Would have been.* As in, Emma would never have that birthday. Her answer only generated more questions, but she didn't slow down long enough to let him ask.

She led him into the main cabin where he grabbed his bags and followed her down a narrow hallway with doors on either side. She stopped at one near the end and knocked.

The man Jack remembered as Mac opened the door, wearing nothing but a pair of shorts. "Hey, Dr. Rhoades, what's up?"

She stepped back.

Mac's gaze landed on Jack. Immediately, his eyes narrowed. "What are you doing here?"

"Mac," Dr. Rhoades said, "Jack accepted the job. He'll provide security to our staff on board the *Nightingale* and when we go ashore to set up our clinics. Because you have the only spare bed on board, you have a new roommate."

Mac opened his mouth to protest, and then clamped it shut without saying a word. With a glare aimed at Jack, he stepped aside.

"I'll leave you two to get to know each other. We leave for shore at seven tomorrow morning." Dr. Rhoades turned and walked away.

Jack's gaze followed her until she disappeared into her own stateroom, noting its location.

"Touch her and I'll kill you," Mac

growled.

At the threat, Jack turned to Mac. "Excuse me?"

"You heard me." Mac entered the room ahead of Jack. "She's one of the nicest, most sincere individuals you'll ever meet. If you hurt her in any way, I'll make sure you regret it."

"Message received." Jack stashed his bags in a locker.

Mac cleared clothes and books off the spare bed. "It's all yours. The head is right across the hallway. Take quick showers as we all have to get one. We're limited on the amount of fresh water we can use so daily stops to fill the tanks aren't required."

"I'll keep that in mind." Jack dug in his duffle, unearthing his shaving kit from the top where he'd stashed it. He stepped across the hall and into the small bathroom equipped with a toilet and a shower. In less than five minutes, he showered the salt off his body and brushed his teeth.

Back in the room with Mac, he lay across the bed, wearing shorts and nothing else. "So, what's your story?" he asked Mac.

"What story?"

"Prior Army?" Jack asked.

"Yeah. So?"

"I recognized the military bearing. Were you a medic?"

"Yeah." Mac lay out on his bed and

tucked his hands behind his head, still stiff, but seeming to bend slightly.

Jack relaxed. Finding common ground helped establish rapport. Their military backgrounds gave them that common ground. "How many tours to the sandbox?"

"One to Iraq, three to Afghanistan. I left the service after the last deployment to Afghanistan."

"Why?"

"Got tired of watching my friends die. I wanted to go where I could do some good."

Jack turned on his side and propped himself up on his elbow. "How did you end up on the *Nightingale*?"

"What is this, twenty questions?" Mac hit the light switch over his bunk.

With the light still shining over Jack's bunk, he could see Mac's facial expressions. The man frowned and he glared at Jack's light.

"I was just curious." Jack reached up and hit the off switch, plunging the room into pitch black. "Dr. Rhoades would inspire most anyone to work for her."

"Damn right. She's got a heart of gold." After a moment or two, he spoke again. "I met her when I volunteered for a trip to Africa with Doctors Without Borders. She did amazing things with those kids. But she never seemed to stay in one place. When her time was up, she gave me her phone number and told me to get in touch when I finished my time with DWB, that she had an idea she was working on."

"And this was her idea?"

"Yeah. She'd already bought the boat and had hired someone to set up a nonprofit organization to collect money to fund the project. I helped her get the contacts to stock the medications and equipment we could afford and would need immediately."

"She's one determined lady," Jack observed.

"You don't know the half of it. When kids are involved she's like a mama bear, willing to fight fiercely for their welfare."

Jack wanted to ask about Emma, but kept his mouth shut. He'd get her to tell him her story, given time. Something he might have little of. If the guerillas came after the floating doctors boat, his job aboard might end before he got all the answers he wanted.

Natalie lay on her bed, her thoughts running in every direction, but coming back to one thing—Jack's kiss. For such a nonsexual kiss, it had rekindled a longing she thought long past with the death of her husband and child.

For the past four and a half years, she'd done everything in her power to keep moving. If she stopped for too long, she was reminded of how lonely life could be. Surrounded by her crew and people she cared about, she shouldn't be lonely. But she was. Before she'd lost everything, she'd had it all. The perfect house in the right neighborhood, nestled in the mountains just north of Denver.

Natalie had married Andrew straight out of college and they both attended the same medical school. When they'd finished, they'd secured internships at the same hospital and months later, she'd gotten pregnant. She finished up her internship and had her baby a few days later. Her whole life had seemed to be on a set course, everything falling into place as if it had been calculated down to the day and hour. Until fate placed them next to an eighteen-wheeler that tragic day.

Her well-ordered life crashed and burned like the car she'd been riding in. Now she was thousands of miles and several years away from that event and thinking about another man, not her dead husband. What was it about Jack that made her want something she had told herself she'd never have again? Held in his arms, she'd felt secure, cared for and protected. Part of her craved more of the same. The other part valued her independence far too much to allow herself to become dependent again on someone for her happiness.

As she thought more about Jack, she realized she really knew nothing about him. Who was he, where did he come from? What were his credentials? She'd been very selective of the people who'd applied for the positions on her boat. She'd done background checks and screened them thoroughly.

So, why had she been so adamant about hiring Jack without any of that? She could have unwittingly brought a pirate or a serial killer on board the *Nightingale* and placed her entire team at risk.

Natalie sat up straight in bed, her pulse pounding. She couldn't go to sleep thinking she might have sabotaged her own crew. Throwing back her sheets, she swung her feet to the floor and stood. She opened the door to her stateroom and peered out into the hallway. What could she do? If she marched down to his room, what would she say?

"Natalie, are you having trouble sleeping?"

The voice next to her made her jump. She pressed a hand to her chest and spun to face Ronnie. "You scared the crap out of me."

"Sorry. You looked confused. I hear you hired Jack."

"I did, but then I realized I don't know anything about him." Her gaze shifted to the door at the end of the hallway.

"Having second thoughts?"

Natalie nodded.

"If it helps, my gut says he can be trusted."

Natalie smiled. "And your gut is always right."

"I've avoided many storms because of my gut." She laid a hand on Natalie's shoulder. "He seemed to be a good guy."

Natalie nodded. "My gut tells me the same. But if I'm wrong, who gets hurt?"

"Trust your instincts. Over the past couple of years, you've led this motley crew well."

"Thank you. I couldn't have done it without you." She touched Ronnie's arm.

"Go to bed. I can sleep with one ear open and keep an eye on our friend Jack."

"You have to work all day tomorrow."

Ronnie grinned. "I can catch some winks after you and the medical team go ashore."

"If you're sure…" Natalie hesitated, still feeling as if she should march down the hallway and demand to know Jack's intentions. But if he were out to destroy them, he wouldn't tell them. He'd lie and slice their throats in the middle of the night.

"Go to bed, doctor." Ronnie turned her around and aimed her toward her stateroom.

Natalie entered and closed the door behind her. Everything would be all right. It had to be. Despite her misgivings, she fell into a deep sleep and, for the first time in four years, didn't have a single nightmare about the crash.

When she woke, daylight streamed through the porthole. She sat up straight in her bed and checked her clock. It was already past the time she normally woke. If she didn't hurry, she'd be late. Hopping out of bed, she landed on bare feet and ran for her closet, pulling out a fresh set of scrubs.

A knock sounded at her door.

"Coming!" she called out and jerked open the door.

Jack Fischer leaned against the doorframe, a sexy smile curling his lips. "The skiff is loaded except for the most important thing."

"Oh, yeah?" she said, pulling her hair up by the handful. "What's that?" She dropped a strand and cursed.

"You. Here, let me do that." He reached for a brush on the built-in dresser. "Turn."

She complied and he worked the brush through the tangles until all were smoothed away, then he pulled it up into a ponytail. "I'll take that band."

Handing him the elastic band she kept on her wrist, she waited while he expertly applied it to her hair, securing it in the back at the nape of her neck. "Thank you." She hugged her scrubs to her chest. "If you don't mind, it will only take me a moment." Pushing him through the door, she shut it in his face and leaned against it, her pulse pounding and her breath lodged in her chest.

Jack Fischer was too much man, muscle and sexiness for that early in the morning. He'd caught her off guard and made her want to drag him into her bed. Her mind conjured an image of them lying naked in her bed, rocking the boat.

Holy crap! Where had that thought come from? He was her employee, not a potential sex partner.

In less than twenty seconds, she'd stripped off the T-shirt and shorts she'd worn to bed, clipped on a bra and pulled her scrubs over her head. Pants went on next and socks and shoes. Fully dressed and ready to go, Natalie grabbed her bag and jerked the door open.

"I'll take that." Jack grabbed her bag and shoved a fat biscuit in her hand. "Eat." He handed her a cup of coffee. "You can drink on your way to the boat."

"I can wait to eat when I get back."

"That will be at the end of the day, and you won't last that long if you don't eat now."

The biscuit and coffee smelled so good, she couldn't decide which to try first. "I've gone all day without food just fine."

"You serve the people better if you follow your own advice and fuel your body."

"True." She took a bit of the biscuit and moaned as she chewed and swallowed. "You didn't tell me it was full of eggs and cheese."

"You were too busy arguing for me to get a word in edgewise. Are you always this disagreeable in the morning?"

Natalie frowned. "I'm not disagreeable,

and I'm always on time."

"Except this morning? Must be the company you keep."

"Definitely." Giving him a challenging look, she bit into the biscuit again, loving every delicious bite. She had to admit, she'd gotten lax about eating breakfast, and lunch was usually hit or miss—more miss than hit, as busy as they were. There always seemed to be more patients than they had time for and Natalie hated to turn away a single one. Thank goodness Mac was so good about triaging the badly injured or sick and letting her see them first.

By the time she reached the little skiff, the others were in it, the small folding table and camp chairs stowed in the bottom.

Natalie had swallowed the last bite of her biscuit, grateful to wash it down with several swigs of coffee. "Are we ready?"

"Ready," Hallie and Mac said in unison.

"Any sign of our friends from yesterday?" Natalie asked.

"None so far," Jack answered. "I checked through binoculars, the shoreline appears clear. I'll scope it out again once we're on land."

"Thank you." Natalie noted he wore cargo pants and a gray T-shirt. The pockets appeared laden with something. She leaned close and whispered, "Are you packing?"

Jack burst out laughing. "Packing?"

She frowned. "You know, carrying a gun." She barely moved her lips so as not to alarm the others waiting in the boat.

He tilted toward her and placed his lips close to her ear. "If I were packing, would it make me sexier?"

Her cheeks burned. Damn it, the thought of Jack carrying a gun both frightened and titillated her, and the fact that he knew it made the situation even worse.

The man was far too attractive for her concentration. How was she supposed to work with him hanging around? His muscles stretched the gray T-shirt tight around his biceps and across his massive chest. Though the cargo pants were supposed to be baggy, his muscular thighs stretched those too.

Jack handed Natalie's bag to Mac and helped her into the boat. As soon as she was seated, Mac started the engine and Jack shoved the skiff away from the *Nightingale*.

Mac handled the rudder at the back of the boat and Hallie smiled, her cheerful self. The sun shone in a clear blue sky, laying sparkling crystals across the water.

Jack climbed onto the jet ski, switched it on, tossed the line onto the boat and spun around.

God, he was beautiful with the shaggy blond hair blowing back, tanned, healthy skin and eyes so blue they rivaled the sea and sky. But his powerful build and air of confidence were what made her body tremble whenever he was near.

*Focus on the shore, Natalie.*

A gathering of locals waited at the water's edge. When the skiff slid onto the sand, eight women grabbed the edges and hauled it up farther on land before anyone could get out.

Those who greeted them reached into the boat and gathered the camp chairs and folding table, carrying them across the sand. They led the team along a short path through the jungle into a small village of huts and ramshackle housing built of anything they found available from old wooden crates to tacked-on tarp. Each sported a thatched roof, made of palm fronds lashed together. In the middle of the village was a small open area.

The villagers set up the table and camp chairs there. Someone brought out a ragged tarp and fixed it to long poles, stretching it over the tables and chairs to provide sufficient shade from the hot sun.

Mac and Hallie performed a preliminary triage, identifying those needing to see the doctor immediately and those that could be helped without the doctor's assistance. The routine was the way they worked. Villagers seemed to come out of the shadows. It never ceased to amaze Natalie that so many people could live in such tiny houses with so few belongings. But they did and the children, though dirty and sometimes malnourished, seemed happy with their lives.

Why couldn't she be as happy?

She glanced up, seeking the newest member of her team. Jack was nowhere to be seen. He'd said he'd check the surroundings closer to be certain no one would surprise them by carrying guns and shooting.

The longer he stayed out of sight, the more worried she became.

Once they hit shore, Jack faded into the undergrowth and searched the nearby jungle for any sign of guerilla activity. Finding nothing along the shoreline, he circled the village, moving quietly through the shadows. At times, he stopped and listened. Nothing seemed out of place, and he didn't see anyone lurking on the perimeter, waiting to pounce on the medical team.

When he was fairly certain the village was free of commandos, he touched the communication device in his ear. "Are you there?"

"About time you checked in," Gator said. "What's going on?"

"We've set up a clinic in a small village close to the shore. You should be able to pick me up on GPS."

"Gotcha," Swede confirmed.

"I'm not sure what to expect. With yesterday's aerial pyrotechnics, I don't know if the guerillas will stick out their necks today. I learned we will be in the town of Trujillo tomorrow to work in their hospital clinic and also tomorrow night. The city has a festival going on, and some members of the team will be in attendance."

"I take it you'll be going along with them?" Gator questioned.

"Dr. Rhoades has expressed an interest in going. I'll be with her."

"Tough duty, right?" Swede laughed.

"We'll organize a ground support team to intermingle at the festival," Gator said. "If the guerillas decide overt ops are too risky with a squadron of Black Hawks performing a military exercise nearby, they might try to sneak in and capture your medical folks during the festival."

Jack's chest tightened. He'd had the same thought, but hearing it from his team made that event feel even more likely. "Having the team at the festival will be good. The guerillas might take any medical staff they can get their hands on." Jack vowed to be right next to Natalie the entire evening. Not for a moment would he let her out of his sight. Too much could happen in a crowded marketplace.

"We're on it," Gator said.

Jack turned back toward the village and almost tripped over a young boy, standing behind him.

The boy stared at him, frowning.

Jack could imagine he appeared peculiar

as if speaking to no one. He bent to the child and spoke in Spanish. "Do you ever talk to yourself?"

His eyes wide, the boy shook his head.

"Well, I do, when I want to think through something difficult." He dug in his pocket for a peppermint candy and held it out. "Do you know who the Castillo Commandos are?"

The boy's eyes grew even wider and he nodded.

So, the guerillas had made their presence known to the village, and the boy's obvious fear indicated the experience hadn't been pleasant.

"I will give you this sweet if you promise to watch for the Commandos and run as fast as you can to tell me if they are coming." He caught the boy's gaze and held it. "Can you do that?"

The boy eyed the candy and nodded his head.

Jack took the boy's hand and closed it around the candy. "You're a good boy."

When he let go of the boy's hand, the child disappeared into the trees and brush.

After another quick circle around the village, Jack returned to the makeshift tent and assisted the doctor, nurse and medic with the growing crowd of patients.

They worked all day and well into the afternoon, nonstop. The villagers offered food to the team. Jack noted Natalie smiled and took the food, but didn't eat, continuing to work with the patients, obviously determined to see each and every one.

Every hour, Jack checked the perimeter, running into the little boy on several occasions.

The boy reported that he hadn't seen the commandos and that he was still watching.

As they began breaking down the clinic, a man arrived from a distant village limping with a nasty, fresh laceration, bruises and a swollen eye.

Jack found him entering the village along a dirt road that led deeper into the interior.

The man could barely walk, he was bleeding and cowered when Jack hurried forward to help him.

Jack had him sit beneath a tree while he applied a pressure bandage over the laceration. Then he told him to stay where he was for a moment while he checked the area. Moving at the edge of the trees, Jack scouted along the road in the direction the man had come. The situation didn't feel right. The victim had obviously been beaten and stabbed recently. A quarter of a mile back, he found tire tracks in the mud and a dark stain on the ground as if someone had bled there.

Senses on alert, he hurried back to the man beneath the tree and helped him into the village where the clinic had been set up.

The crowd had thinned to only a couple of minor injuries, ear infections and sniffles.

Jack helped the man to the chair in front of Natalie. "I found him on the road leading out of the village. I have a feeling he was injured on purpose. We need to wrap it up soon. If the guerillas did this, they aren't far from here."

Natalie's lips thinned and she gave a slight nod, then she went to work on the victim's injuries. She cleaned the wound, speaking in a soft, soothing voice as she pulled out a syringe and filled it with a local anesthetic.

The man's eyes widened and he started to rise.

Dr. Rhoades touched his arm with her free hand. She patiently explained what was in the syringe and how it would help with the pain while she sewed his wound.

After several long minutes, the man collapsed in the chair and watched as she applied the local along the undamaged edges of the skin around the wound.

Within minutes, she had the wound stitched and a bandage applied. She told the man how to care for it and to boil water and let it cool before cleaning the wound to avoid infection.

While she worked, the team finished up with the other patients and asked the villagers to carry camp chairs to the skiff.

Jack alternated between being in the village and watching the dirt road.

The injured man thanked her profusely and limped back the way he'd come.

"We need to go," Jack said.

"On our way." Dr. Rhoades stood, gathered her bag and reached for the camp chair.

A local woman snatched it up and carried it to the waiting boat.

Jack waited at the tree line until the last minute to ward off any attacks, giving the crew on the boat enough time to get out. He was edgy, feeling as though something wasn't right. The people of the village who had been there to greet their arrival had disappeared without the usual send off. Jack stood in the shadows, watching the trail, shifting his gaze to anything that made a sound.

By the time the skiff was on the water and headed to the boat, the sun angled toward the horizon, getting close to the treetops and casting long shadows across the beach.

Jack was about to run for his jet ski when a tug on his cargo pants pocket made him jump.

The little boy he'd given a mint to earlier appeared beside him, stepping out from the shadows.

His pulse pounding, he turned to the kid who had a future as a guerilla fighter—silent and stealthy.

Squatting to get on eyelevel with the boy, Jack dug in his pocket for another mint.

The boy glanced back over his shoulder. In Spanish, he said, "The commandos, they are watching." He grabbed the mint and ducked back into the forest, disappearing in seconds.

Jack checked the boat. No one had come out of the woods to chase it down, and the gunboat from the day before didn't materialize.

If they were watching, what were they waiting on? Had they figured out they were being watched by the unit of Black Hawks supposedly on a military exercise? Whatever it was, Jack felt like a target as he stepped out from the shadows to cross the open beach. He walked quickly, wondering when the bullets would hit him in the back. He reached the jet ski, shoved it out into the water and jumped on.

Nothing. No bullets, no gunfire. No guerillas rushed out to grab him or the medical team. He raced out over the water, but his skin crept so he swerved back and forth so that he could glance back at the shoreline. With the shadows deepening, he could see nothing moving beneath the trees. He didn't feel comfortable until they were all on board.

Dr. Rhoades hurried to the pilothouse.

Jack followed. "Let's move."

Ronnie frowned. "Run into trouble?"

The doctor shook her head. "No, but I felt creepy there at the last. As though we were being watched." Frowning, she turned to Jack. "Did you see anything?"

"Nothing, but I had the same feeling. If it was the guerillas, why didn't they attack?"

Ronnie started the engines and pushed the throttle forward. "I don't know but it's time to move out."

Dr. Rhoades gaze met Jack's. "The sooner, the better."

# Chapter Four

Natalie poured a glass of wine and walked out on the deck. She stood at the railing, staring out at the moonlight skimming across the water. For the past five years, she'd performed the same ritual. She drank a toast to her daughter's memory, also hoping to dull the ache with a little bit of alcohol. "Happy birthday, Emma," she said to the stars. Then she tipped her glass and took a sip.

"Happy birthday, Emma," a low, resonant voice echoed her words.

Natalie didn't turn. She could feel his presence and knew who was nearby without having to look. Jack stepped up to where she stood and leaned his elbows on the railing. He wore shorts and a loose tank that did little to cover his massive chest, and he was barefoot like her.

"What was she like?" he asked.

With Jack standing close, Natalie didn't feel as alone as she usually did. She didn't even feel like crying. She'd done enough of that the night before. Instead, she sipped her wine and let the good memories of her daughter flow over her and remind her she'd been her mom for eight happy months. "She was a good baby. She slept through the night from the second month on."

"How long did you have her?"

The knot in her chest tightened and she swallowed hard. "Eight months."

Jack shook his head. "Too short."

"Yeah." She sipped more wine, the effect of the alcohol making her tingle. Or was the reaction because of the man standing next to her? Either way, the sensation took the edge off her grief, and for that, she was grateful.

"What happened, or is it too painful to talk about?"

Natalie shrugged. "It's been over four years. You would think it would be easier by now."

"Losing someone you care about is never easy." He stared out at the water, his face grim.

His expression appeared as if he spoke from experience. Natalie stared at him, wondering yet again, who this man was she'd hired onto her boat. She sensed there was so much more to him than a deckhand for hire. "Have you lost someone you cared about?"

Jaw muscles clenched and he nodded. "Two of my brothers."

Natalie touched his arm. "I'm sorry."

"Me, too. They were good men. Strong, smart and dedicated."

"You must miss them."

With a narrowed gaze, he stared out across the water. "Every day."

"Were you close?"

"I'd have given my life for them."

Natalie stood in silence, her heart beating faster. She felt a connection to this man through shared grief. All the pent-up guilt and emotion she'd locked away since her husband's and baby Emma's deaths relaxed.

"She was a happy baby and was just learning to walk when the accident happened."

"House or vehicular?"

"Run off the road by an eighteen-wheeler," Natalie said the statement out loud, amazed that she didn't choke in the middle. Talking felt good, like liberating her heart. "We were on the way to visit my husband's parents in Denver."

"And your husband?" Jack asked.

Her lips twisted. "When the car rolled, their seatbelts held, they stayed with the vehicle all the way to the bottom of the hill. I was thrown clear after the first roll. For years, I've told myself that I hope they died immediately in the crash."

"Why?"

"The car exploded into flame. I couldn't bear to think they were still alive when that happened." Her body shook as once again, the memory of the flames burned through her soul.

Jack's arms slipped around her. "I'm sorry. You must have loved them so very much. There're no words that can ease that memory. I know."

She leaned her cheek against his chest "I could do nothing. I came to long enough to see the flames, then passed out again. I should have been in that car with them." She could feel Jack shaking his head.

"No," he said. "You had more to do in this life."

"Emma and Andrew didn't?" She leaned back. "Andrew was interning to be a heart surgeon. I think of all the lives he could have saved. And Emma, who knows what her life would have been. She'll never go to kindergarten, never fall in love, never give me grandchildren. She should have had a life. But she didn't." Natalie pressed her cheek to his chest, her eyes dry, her heart full of what could have been.

"Nothing I can say will change that. But you are a talented physician. You have so much to give to others. I watched the people of that village come to you with their sick and injured." He smoothed a hand over her head. "You gave them hope."

She nodded. "Knowing my work makes a difference is the only reason I can keeping going."

"Dr. Rhoades, there is no doubt that you make a difference to the people you serve." He tipped up her head and stared down into her eyes.

"Natalie," she whispered, her gaze dropping to his lips. "You can call me Natalie."

"Natalie," he said, the sound rumbling in his chest. "The truth is that you lived. You can't beat yourself up for what happened. Second-guessing whether or not you put your seatbelt on right or if you'd left a little earlier won't change what happened."

His reassuring words vibrated against her ear and she sighed. "I know."

"You have to go on living."

"Even when I feel like something really important died inside?"

"Don't you see? They didn't die inside you. They still live inside you. That's why you will never forget who they were or the joy they brought you when they were still here on earth."

"You're right." Natalie smiled up at him. "How did you get to be so insightful?"

His brushed a stray strand of her hair behind her ear. "When life knocks me around, I don't believe in giving up. And neither do you." He kissed the tip of her nose. "Do you know when the moonlight reflects off your eyes, I feel like I can see all the way into your soul?"

She laughed. "You're a deckhand and a poet? Do you charge extra for flattery—"

He cut off her words with a kiss, his mouth claiming hers in a gentle, but insistent touch.

Almost five years had gone by since she'd wanted to kiss anyone. Now, she found herself wanting to kiss Jack. Again and again. The last kiss she'd shared with Andrew had been a quick goodnight kiss the night before he'd died.

Jack's kisses were completely different, stirring emotions and sensations she thought long dead and buried with her first husband. Her pulse raced, and her core awoke and burned low in her belly.

In a single kiss, he reminded her she was alive and healthy and had needs she'd long ignored. The conditions were right with the moon shining bright in the tropical sky, the sea bathed in sparkling diamonds, reflecting the light in the sky and a soft breeze stirring her hair across her skin, tickling her nerves to life. Warm tropical air wrapped around her and him, making her glad she wore nothing but a soft, stretchy pair of shorts and a tank top. Thinking she'd be alone, she'd forgone the bra—glad now that she had, and that she wasn't alone.

Rather than draw away and act affronted at his kiss, Natalie leaned up on her toes and returned it. At the touch of his tongue tracing the line of her lips, she opened to him, allowing him in.

She raised her hands, circling his neck, drawing him closer. Her body pressing against his hard lines absorbed his heat and strength. A surge of something like power roared through her when she felt the hard ridge of his member nudging her belly. It ignited a flame inside that burned brighter by the minute.

Natalie couldn't slow her heart, couldn't catch her breath, and she didn't want to break the contact. Emboldened by the darkness, she lifted her foot and slid her calf along his.

Jack shifted, his knee slipping between hers, his muscled thigh pressing against her center.

With both of them wearing nothing but shorts and tank tops, there was little standing between their naked skin.

Shifting the kiss from her mouth, Jack blazed a path along her neck down to the pulse beating at the base of her throat.

Tingles running along her skin, Natalie tipped her head to give him better range and ran her hands down his chest to the hem of his shirt. She wanted to touch him, skin-to-skin, to feel just how hard those muscles were. She climbed her fingers over his taut abs and up his torso.

He worked his lips down to her shoulder, nipping and flicking her skin, while his hands slipped lower down her sides. His thumbs brushed over her breasts.

Natalie sucked in a breath and arched her back, pressing her chest against his, her hands caught between them.

Then he bent and scooped the backs of her thighs into his big hands, wrapping her legs around his waist. He turned and backed her against the wall of the cabin, taking her into the darkest shadows, away from possible prying eyes. There, he kissed her again, the gentle brush of his lips a faint memory as he crushed her mouth with his and took her breath away.

After pulling her arms loose, Natalie grabbed the back of his shirt and yanked it over his head, dropping it to the ground.

Jack leaned back enough to tear her tank up over her head to join his at their feet. Her pale skin glowed in the darkness. Because they were in the shadows, she couldn't read his expression as he stared down at her naked breasts. For a long moment, he held her without taking more.

Her skin prickled and her nipples tightened into hard little beads. Her breath lodged in her throat as she waited for some indication of his thoughts. About the time she believed he might have changed his mind, she heard him speak.

"You're beautiful." He cupped one of her breasts, lifting it with his palm.

She let go of the breath she'd been holding and laughed softly. "You're not so bad yourself." She smoothed a hand over his shoulders, loving the difference between his hard body and her soft one. "I was beginning to think you'd changed your mind."

"Oh, hell no." He squeezed the breast gently between his fingers and thumbed the nipple. "I could look at you all night long and not get enough."

"Are you sure you're not a poet?" Pulse racing, she wrapped her hands around his neck and drew him close. "Because you say the nicest things."

"Nothing but the truth. You're an amazing woman." His lips touched hers briefly and then he dropped her legs to the ground and turned. "And, regrettably, I can't do this. You deserve better."

Disappointment hit her full in the chest. She stood behind him, the warm tropical air kissing her naked skin, arousing her even more as she stared at Jack's broad shoulders. "Better what?"

"A soft bed, roses, respect and hours of foreplay." He didn't face her as he spoke, his hands clenched into tight fists.

Her heart fluttered. He was fighting himself not to touch her. That power surged inside her. Taking a step forward, she wrapped her hands around his middle, pressing her naked breasts to his equally naked back. God, he felt good. "What if I don't want better? What if I want here and now?" She slid her hands down his flat belly and inside the elastic waistband of his shorts.

He sucked in a breath and his cock surged upward into her hands. "You have a chance to walk away. Take it," he said, his voice harsh, his body so tense he was like a bowstring pulled too tight, ready to blast free.

"I don't want to walk away." She wrapped her fingers around his member and slid them lower to the base and back up again. "Can't we pretend we're alone in the middle of the ocean? Just you and me. Nothing else matters. Unless—" Her hands froze. "Oh hell. Unless you're worried I'll fire you. Damn. I'm sorry. For a moment I forgot, I'm your boss." She started to pull away.

His hand captured hers on his member, holding her there. "I'm not worried about that. If the situation bothers you, I can fix that."

"How?"

He turned and pulled her against him. "I quit."

"But you can't quit. We still need you to provide security."

"You can hire me tomorrow. Tonight, I'm just a man, holding a beautiful woman in the moonlight."

"But why did you hesitate if not because you were afraid of losing your job?"

A finger ran along her jaw as he stared down at her.

She rested her hands on his chest, feeling the rapid beat of his heart against her fingertips.

"You've lost enough," he said at last. "Whatever happens between us will most likely be temporary. I don't know where the wind will blow me next. I can't make you any guarantees. And I like you enough that I couldn't stand to bring you more pain than you've already experienced."

She pressed a finger to his lips. "Shut up and let me talk."

He kissed her finger and grinned. "Yes, ma'am."

Natalie steeled herself to be open and honest. "I've been wallowing in the past for so long, I didn't know how to think of a future. I've taken life one day at a time, doing what I know how to do, living but not really feeling alive. For the first time in years, I feel alive." She smiled, her heart lighter than it had been in a long time. "I've learned one thing through it all—life gives us no guarantees. You take what you can, when you can, because the opportunity might not be there tomorrow." She cupped his cheek in her palm, enjoying the rough prickle of beard stubble. "I choose to take what I can tonight. If you're here tomorrow, I'll count that as a blessing. If you aren't, I'll have tonight to remember."

Determined to make a sizzling hot memory, she kissed his lips as she guided his hand up to her breast.

Jack fought for control, but his body overrode him. One hand curved around her breast, the other slid lower to the elastic waistband of her shorts. He hooked his fingers and dragged them down her legs and off, kissing his way back up.

She did the same to him, sliding his shorts down his legs, careful not to disturb his bandage, her hands gliding over his skin on the way down, her lips on the way back up.

He couldn't get any harder.

In the shadow of the cabin, in a secluded corner of the deck, they stood naked, nothing but the tropical air between their bodies.

Of all the places he'd been, this was the one place he'd remember the most. Not because of the ocean lapping against the side of the ship or the moonlight streaming across the water, but because of this woman, whose heart had been broken. She'd found the courage to move on and give back to a world that had taken so much.

He gathered her in his arms, realizing what a special person she was and that what they were about to do would be extraordinary. When his skin touched hers, he lost all semblance of control. He backed her up to the wall and pressed his cock against her mound, eager to be inside her, to take her hard and fast. If he were a gentleman, he'd make the time to get her hot and slick.

Oh, hell, he wanted her as aroused as he was. He bent and took one of her breasts in his mouth and suckled, flicking the tip and rolling the nipple between his teeth.

Sucking in a breath, she curled her hand around the back of his head, her fingers twisting in his hair. She arched her back, giving him more. When he'd thoroughly teased that breast, she guided him to the other. "Please," she begged, urging him to treat the other in the same arousing way.

He tasted, nibbled and teased the nipple into a tight little bud before he swept down her torso to the apex of her thighs. She spread her legs wider, giving him better access to part her folds and strum that center strip of sensitized flesh with the flick of his finger until she moaned.

Natalie rocked her hips, her fingers digging into his scalp, pulling him away one second and urging him to take more in the next.

Jack leaned in and tapped her clit with the tip of his tongue.

Her body froze, tensed, waiting.

With a slow stroke, he licked the length of it and sucked it into his mouth, the fresh, musky taste of her making him want to rise to his feet and plunge deep inside her body. But he played her, stroking her until her entire body trembled and she dragged at his hair to make him quit. He refused to let up, slowing his tongue strokes to long soothing swirls.

She moaned and rocked her hips, her fingers pulling at his hair as her body pulsed her climax, her legs trembling in his palms.

A surge of power rammed through Jack. He'd done this. He'd brought her to brink and pushed her over.

When she reached for his arms and pulled at him to rise, he came to his feet and lifted her, wrapping her legs around his waist.

He eased her down over him, entering her in on long, fluid thrust.

When she was fully seated, he froze, his hands digging into her hips. "Oh, God, we forgot protection."

"It's okay," she said. "Unless you have some STDs." She leaned her forehead against his, her breathing ragged. "Tell me you don't."

"I'm clean."

"And I'm equipped with an IUD."

"You're sure you're okay with this? I'll stop, if you want." He sucked in a shaky breath. "At least, I think I can stop."

"For the love of Mike, don't stop." She raised herself up and lowered herself onto him again. "This feels entirely too good to stop now. Make me howl at the moon, Jack. I'm long overdue."

Pressing her back against the wall of the cabin, he held her hips in his hands and pounded into her again and again, the tension building inside until he burned all over. Just.

One. Last. Thrust…and he catapulted into the stratosphere, burying himself as deep as he could go. He held her hips until his member quit throbbing, and he could take a deep breath.

Natalie smoothed her hands up over his arms and shoulders and captured his cheeks. "Now that wasn't so hard, was it?"

Harder than she could imagine. When he'd started down this path, he had kept in mind that he was a SEAL, on missions more often than he was home and not good boyfriend or husband material.

Natalie was the type of woman who needed a man to keep her safe…and satisfied on a more regular basis.

He wasn't that man. But, oh how he wanted to be.

# Chapter Five

Natalie woke early the next morning, her body energized from great sex and the best night's sleep she'd had in a very long time. She hadn't had any nightmares, in fact, she'd dreamed Jack had slept in the bed beside her, making love to her all night long. Alas, it was only a dream.

After they'd made passionate love on the deck of the *Nightingale*, he'd helped her dress and escorted her to her stateroom where he'd kissed her goodnight and walked away.

She could have kicked herself for not inviting him in to stay the night. But then again, he would have given her some indication that he wanted to, wouldn't he? With the light of day streaming through the porthole of her stateroom, Natalie wondered how she would face the man, now that they'd made love. Would seeing him be awkward, especially because she couldn't touch him? Would the rest of the crew figure out the truth by the crazy grin on her face when she stepped out into the sunshine?

Natalie crawled out of bed, her breasts sensitive to the touch, having been tongued, nibbled and sucked last night. She had a deliciously sexy ache between her legs from making love with Jack.

She glanced in the mirror at the color flying high like flags in her cheeks. Holy shit, had she really made love on the deck of the *Nightingale*? What if one of her crew had seen her? What if Jack quit for real and had left the boat that morning?

That thought made her dress in record time. She jerked a brush through her hair and slapped it up in a ponytail. Thank goodness, no time at all was needed to throw on a pair of scrubs. A quick toothbrush over her teeth and water splashed in her face and she was done with her usual morning ritual. Should she put on some mascara and lip gloss? She reached for the gloss and her hand froze in midair. "No. He kissed you without lip gloss both times. It wasn't the lip gloss he was attracted to."

Her body tingled and she shivered from top to toe.

He was attracted to her.

After slipping on her tennis shoes, she tied them and ran out the door to find Jack. In a quick flyby of the galley, she snatched a bagel and determined Jack wasn't there or in the dining area. Out on deck, she ran into the entire team, preparing the skiff for the day's clinic at the hospital in Trujillo.

"Craig, how are you feeling this morning?" she asked, her gaze shooting past everyone, searching for Jack.

"Much better, thank you." He set the case of medications and bandages into the bottom of the boat and straightened. "We'll need all hands on deck to handle the mob in Trujillo."

"Especially since the annual festival happens today," Hallie grinned. "We will have time to come back to the boat to change, won't we?"

"Yes, Hallie, we'll quit early enough to partake in the festivities." Natalie smiled. "I'm looking forward to the music and dancing."

Mac glowered. "We won't have time to return here and take a nap before we have to turn around and head back into the town tonight."

"That's okay," Hallie sang, her personality bubbling over. "All we need is to clean up and change into party clothes."

"Some of us got more sleep than others," Mac said, his gaze seeking Natalie's.

She met his accusing stare straight on, her stomach knotting. "I got plenty of sleep. Did you, Mac?"

He pulled her to the side. "I know what happened last night out on the deck."

Though heat rose up her neck into her cheeks, Natalie managed to keep her expression level, unaffected. "Is that so? And why is that? Was it because you couldn't sleep? I can prescribe a sleep aid if you need one."

"I don't need a sleep aid." Mac gripped her arms. "I don't trust him and you shouldn't either."

"If you're talking about Jack, you'll have to be more specific as to why you don't trust him."

"Did you know he carries guns in his cargo pockets?"

"I certainly hope so. He's in charge of security."

"Well, while you two were up on deck getting it on, I checked through his duffle bag."

Natalie's teeth clenched. "This is a small boat, and one of the unwritten rules is that you have to respect each individual's privacy. You had no right to go through his duffle."

Mac's gaze captured hers. "He's also got a top-of-the-line, breakdown rifle with a high-powered scope tucked in amongst his skivvies."

"So? Again, he's our security."

"Natalie, think about it. Where does a beach bum get a rifle like that? He either got it from a terrorist organization or he stole it."

Natalie bit down hard on her tongue, wanting to refute everything Mac had to say. No, she wanted Jack to tell her where he'd gotten an expensive weapon like that. If she asked him, she'd show that she wasn't firm in her trust in him. And if he had a reasonable explanation, that still wouldn't negate her lack of trust.

Hell, she'd had hot sex on the deck with the man. That took a certain amount of trust. She glanced around, hoping to find Jack before they took off to set up the clinic in Trujillo.

"If you're looking for him, you'll have to look a lot harder. He's already out on his jet ski. That's another anomaly. How did he afford a jet ski if he's a deckhand? The one he's riding is also an expensive model. If you don't believe me, look it up online."

"Mac, we don't have time to go into this. We're due on shore in twenty minutes, and I haven't even loaded my bag."

"I restocked and put it in the boat while you were sleeping in."

"Thank you." When she started to walk away, she felt Mac grab her arm again.

"Natalie, don't get too deep with Fischer. He could be leading you down the garden path, setting you up for some real heartache, whether he's who he says he is or not."

"I'm a big girl. I can take care of myself." She shook off his hand and strode toward the skiff, irritation fueling her steps.

"You're old enough to make your own decisions, but that doesn't stop us from caring about what happens to you," Mac called out after her.

Natalie checked what had been stowed in the boat. They'd need more supplies on this trip because they were close to a decent-sized town. Trujillo had a small but clean hospital with a dedicated staff of one surgeon and a doctor and half a dozen nurses who worked the day and night shifts.

The team from the *Nightingale* would augment the hospital staff and help them in any way possible without trying to take over. For the community to have faith in their own infrastructure was important.

From their reconnaissance mission earlier that year, they learned they would be set up in the hospital clinic, helping with vaccinations with supplies they'd brought for just that purpose. Additional medications to help stock the hospital's meager stores would be distributed.

Satisfied they had what they needed, Natalie settled into the skiff and waited for a sullen Mac to shove off. This time, the entire team would be on hand to lend assistance. The little boat full of supplies and people left the *Nightingale* in the middle of Trujillo Bay and motored across to the tiny port town. Jack provided an escort, riding close, but not close enough for Natalie to see the expression on his face.

She would have liked to talk with him that morning to gauge his reaction to what they had shared the night before. But based on his distance and the fact he hadn't been interested enough to face her that morning, he was probably having second thoughts.

Natalie couldn't deny her disappointment, but she reminded herself she'd accepted the conditions. He wasn't planning on staying forever and she knew life didn't come with guarantees. So, why was she so depressed?

Hell. She'd just have to get over it and focus once again on what she did well.

As they neared the dock, Mac cut the engine and they drifted the rest of the way. A group of children helped tie off the skiff, and Dr. Jimenez greeted them, extending a hand to help Natalie out of the boat onto the weathered wooden planking. "Dr. Rhoades, welcome."

Natalie greeted the man with a smile and a hug. "How are you, Dr. Jimenez?" She would have liked to be less formal, but the good doctor insisted on formality as part of the culture of his little town. Natalie understood the importance of culture and norms and tried to instill the same values and lessons in her team. People, no matter how poor or wealthy, deserved to be treated with respect for whom they are, along with their beliefs and lifestyles.

Jack didn't tie off his jet ski until Natalie and her crew were halfway across the dock. Once again, she would have liked to speak with him before she went to work that day. But then, maybe they'd done all their talking the night before.

Walking through the streets of Trujillo, Natalie smiled at the inhabitants, decorating the outsides of their houses with crepe paper. Colorful, fringed streamers stretched overhead between buildings, fluttering in the breeze. The festival was in honor of the town's patron saint and the locals and tourists enjoyed the festivities for days.

Dr. Jimenez led them through the front door of the Trujillo Hospital and set them up in the tiny clinic and one of the hospital wards. The clinic would see patients needing vaccinations and minor wound care. The hospital ward would be for more extensive wound care and sicknesses. All treatment was advertised as free and, with the festival in town, they expected a large turnout.

The day passed quickly with so many patients the team and the entire hospital staff were constantly busy. By lunch, they'd seen over fifty sick or injured patients and administered hundreds of vaccinations.

Natalie didn't spot Jack until she took a brief break at lunchtime. She stood in the doorway of the hospital, taking a few deep breaths before plunging back into the work. A line of patients sat in the shade, sharing what little food they had.

Jack had commandeered a bucket of water from the hospital and paper cups the team had brought along. He was busy handing out cups of water to those still waiting to be seen. He smiled at the ladies and they smiled back. When they spoke in Spanish, he was quick to chuckle and reply in their language. The children especially loved him, helping him by holding the cups while he poured water into them and laughing when he spilled it on them purposely.

By the time Jack made it back to the door, Natalie was smiling, too.

"I'd say good morning, but it's lunchtime." Jack winked. "Did you sleep well?"

Natalie nodded. "I did. And you?" Her cheeks warmed, and not because of the sun shining down on her. She was surprised at how giddy she felt standing next to him, like a teenager after her first date with the sexy football player. Wanting to press her cool hands against her hot cheeks, she shoved them into her pockets and tried to act as though nothing out of the ordinary had happened, when in her heart she knew her life had actually changed by making love to this man.

"You're blushing," Jack said. "I hope you're not embarrassed by last night, because it was nothing to be embarrassed about. Being together was pure magic." He leaned over and kissed her cheek.

The children around him all giggled and hid their eyes behind their hands.

"Shouldn't you be looking for guerillas or something?" Mac said from behind Natalie.

She sucked in a breath and let it out slowly to keep from turning and glaring at Mac. When she did turn, she smiled. "Let's get back to work."

Mac scowled at Jack.

Jack just smiled at him. "Have you two had lunch?"

Natalie shook her head. "I rarely eat lunch while working with the locals."

Jack dug into a pocket in his cargo pants and pulled out several foil-wrapped protein bars. "I thought so. Take these for an energy boost."

Natalie gave him a wry grin. "Now, who's giving health advice?"

"Simple mechanics. Your body is like an engine. It can't run without fuel." He performed and about-face then hurried down the street and around a corner.

"Something just doesn't jive with that man. He seems to know a lot, but he isn't sharing," Mac said.

Natalie handed him a nutrition bar. "He shared his lunch." She patted Mac's shoulder and entered the hospital to go back to work, ripping into the package. She found herself counting the hours until the day was done and she could see Jack again.

Jack remained in relatively close vicinity

to the hospital in Trujillo, afraid to venture too far and not be on hand should the guerillas attempt another attack on the medical staff. He'd checked in with his team aboard the *Pegasus* that morning once he'd gotten far enough away from the *Nightingale* that he wouldn't be seen doing what would appear like talking to himself.

The team was restless. Gator had been ready to recall him and look in other locations to find the guerilla hideout.

Jack convinced them to give it one more night. After the boy's report the day before and the creepy feeling of being watched, Jack was convinced it was only a matter of time before the Castillo Commandos made their move on the team of medical personnel. He felt positive the Black Hawk support had chased them back into the jungle and their next move would be more covert.

"Fish." A voice called out to him from a shadowy corner between two stucco buildings.

Jack spun to face Gator, the six-foot tall, Louisiana Cajun who'd just gotten himself engaged to a NCIS agent a couple months back. He swore he wasn't quitting the team, but Jack guessed it could happen someday. Marriage and family sometimes made SEALs think twice before committing to the next potentially deadly mission.

Having never met a woman who could

hold up under the pressure of being a Navy SEAL wife and one he could see himself spending the rest of what was left of his life with, Jack hadn't understood the desire to marry.

Until he'd met Natalie. Though he'd only known her a very short time, he could see himself coming home to her every night. She was gentle but tough enough to withstand the worry and uncertainty that went hand-in-hand with being a Navy SEAL wife.

"Where's the rest of the team?" Jack asked, shaking himself out of dreams he had no business dreaming.

"Most are gearing up for tonight's festival," Gator said. "I have Dustman and Irish with me on opposites ends of Trujillo, watching the traffic going in and out of town. How are things with the doctor?"

"What do you mean?" Jack shot a look at Gator. Had he guessed?

Gator's brows rose. "I asked a simple question. What *should* I mean?" He crossed his arms. "Spill. What's going on between you and the pretty doctor lady?"

When an answer didn't come immediately, Gator shook his head. "Please don't tell me you're fucking the bait."

Anger flared and Jack shoved Gator, his superior, up against the wall. "Shut the fuck up about Natalie—Dr. Rhoades. She's classy and she's not like that."

"But you did her? Holy shit, Fish. I send you out to perform a mission of getting in good with the doctor team, not getting *into* the doctor."

"I said, shut the fuck up." Jack shoved a hand through his hair and spun away.

"Sorry, man. It's just that I'm stunned. Two nights on the boat and you're already in her panties. That has to be a record for you."

Jack didn't respond, his focus destroyed. Falling in bed with someone when he was on a mission wasn't like him. He saved that for when he had downtime and needed to let off a little steam. Natalie wasn't stress relief. She was different. "She's amazing," he said on a sigh.

"And when we're done here?"

"I'll still be a SEAL stationed out of Virginia, and she'll still be running a floating doctor boat in some of the poorest countries along the coast of middle and South America."

"Exactly. You're only here for a couple days. Don't get too wrapped around the axels with the good doctor. It will only set you both up for long lonely nights ahead."

Gator was right. Damn him. But he'd taken the plunge and committed to one woman. "How did you know Mitchell was the one for you? Did it take long? Hours? Days? Weeks?"

Gator laughed, his gaze shifting to a wall

in front of him as though he was watching a movie screen playing all his old, favorite memories. "I knew the moment I saw her deck a marine who'd gotten a little too fresh at the bar."

"But you didn't get together that quickly."

"No, Brewsky asked her out first. I was too much of a dumbass to do it. He asked her to marry him before I had a chance and…well, you know the code." He shook his head. "You don't steal your buddy's girl."

"Brewsky's girl." Jack nodded. Brewsky died during one of their missions. Jack was on that one, and watched his friend take the hit.

"So, you're telling me you have feelings for the doctor lady?" Gator's lips thinned. "Are you getting too close to be objective? Do I need to pull you off and put another man inside the medical team?"

"No!" Jack added, "No. I'll be okay. I know whatever this is will go nowhere. We'd never be in the same place again."

"Not unless one or the other of you gives up your day jobs." Gator's brows dipped. "You're not thinking about quitting the Navy, are you?"

"No, I'm a frogman through and through." He sighed again. "It's just that she's…"

"Amazing?" Gator laughed. "I get it. Just know that your brothers will be there to pick up the pieces when you fall apart. Do us a favor, though. Don't fall apart when the Castillo Commandos come callin'."

"Right." He had to maintain focus on his real reason for being there. Stop the guerillas from kidnapping rich yacht owners and holding them for ransom, and to recover the ones they already had. "What's the plan for tonight?"

"Twelve members of the team will be positioned surrounding the perimeter and intermingled in the crowd as tourists. The rest will be manning jet skis and motorboats in the bay, in case the guerillas show up in their gunboat again."

"Good. I want to tell the medical staff to stay on board the *Nightingale,* but if I do that, I have to tell them why."

"And that includes owning up to lying about your real job." Gator patted his back. "I bet your lady doctor wouldn't be too happy about being lied to."

"Probably not." Hell, she'd be furious. "However, if the guerillas make their move tonight, the entire medical team could be in danger of being kidnapped or killed."

"And if they don't make their move tonight, I will recall you, and we have to come up with a different plan to find our target."

Jack nodded. "Understood." His time with Natalie was coming to an end, one way or another. Being together wasn't meant to last to begin with. "I'd better get back to the hospital, they should be closing up shop soon."

"Jack." Gator caught his arm. "We're Navy SEALs, and we're also people with the same needs and desires as others. If both parties are willing and passionate about being together, they'll find a way."

"Thanks, man. Even I can recognize a lose-lose situation when it hits me in the gut." Jack left Gator in the shadows and hurried back to the hospital.

The line of patients had dwindled to two and they were being led in as he arrived.

A few minutes later, they exited with smiles on their faces, thanking Dr. Rhoades and Dr. Biacowski who followed them to the door.

Dr. Jimenez joined them, drying his hands on a towel. "It was a good day. Thank you." He flipped the towel up on his shoulder and held out his hand to Dr. Biacowski and then Dr. Rhoades. "And thank you for the supplies. We rarely have all that we need or when we get it, the medications have already exceeded their expiry dates. *Gracias, amigos.*"

The team packed up their cases that were much lighter than when they'd arrived. Members of the hospital staff helped carry them down to the dock.

Jack fell in beside Natalie, who brought up the rear of the tired crew. "I believe you had some happy patients."

"Some more so than others." She smiled. "Now to get out to the boat, clean up and come back for the festivities." Natalie groaned. "All I want is a shower and bed." Her gaze flicked to the side then straight ahead. "Oh, and a sandwich. By the way, thank you for the protein bar. I would not have made it without its calories today."

"You always come prepared for the patients, but not for yourself. Your health is as important, if not more important than the patients you see. If you let yourself get run down, you will be of no use to the people who rely on you." He waved a hand as he spoke. "Add the fact that a run-down body is more susceptible to disease in a disease-ridden jungle, and you have a dangerous combination."

"Why, Dr. Jack, I don't know why I bothered to get a medical license."

"Sorry, it's all the advice you give your patients. But I've noticed that doctors are their own worst patients."

"You have a point." She dropped her bag in the boat. Dr. Biacowski, Hallie and Steve had already climbed aboard. Mac tapped his foot on the dock.

Jack glanced at his jet ski. "Want to ride with me?"

Natalie glanced from the boat full of her team to the jet ski.

For a moment, Jack thought she would decline his offer. Then she surprised him by saying, "Yes."

Mac glared at Jack. "She needs to ride with the team, and you need to be free to provide security or whatever it is you do."

Jack's gaze didn't leave Natalie's face. "Your choice, Dr. Rhoades."

Natalie's gaze moved from Mac to Jack and back to Mac. "You can transport the team back to the *Nightingale* without me. I'll ride with Jack."

Jack fought hard to contain his grin. Once his back was turned to the others, he let it loose. Natalie was riding with him. He dropped down onto the jet ski and then held onto her hand as she settled onto the back of the seat. While the skiff turned and headed back to the boat, Jack followed at a slow pace behind it.

"Is this as good as it gets?" Natalie yelled over the roar of the engine.

Jack grinned, goosed the throttle and made a wide arc around the skiff. Keeping a careful watch on the bay, searching for guerilla gunboats, he blasted across the water, making sharp turns that had Natalie holding tightly around his middle and laughing out loud. He liked the feel of her arms around him and her laughter brightened his day.

By the time they returned to the *Nightingale*, the others had unloaded the skiff and were headed toward the galley. After Dr. Biacowski's stomach issues, none of them wanted to risk eating on the economy and coming down with an illness or a parasite.

Jack helped Natalie off the jet ski and secured the line.

She waited until he straightened before taking his hand. "Thank you." Then she leaned up on her toes and kissed his lips, barely brushing them with hers.

That simple touch wasn't nearly enough. Jack clamped an arm around her waist and pulled her against him in a breath-stealing, heart-throbbing kiss that would set him back a long way on getting over the beautiful Dr. Rhoades. When he let her go, he whispered, "Save a dance for me."

# Chapter Six

Natalie ran the brush through her hair one last time, pulled a big swath of it up on the left side and clipped it behind her ear, letting the other side fall down in silken waves over her shoulder. Laying the brush on the counter, she stared at herself in the little mirror over her sink. She'd applied mascara, a smoky blue eye shadow Hallie had let her borrow and shiny rose-petal pink lip gloss.

She wore a white peasant blouse with the neckline pulled down on her arms, exposing all of her shoulders the way the woman at the Costa Rican market had showed her. And the flouncy bright red skirt that swung way out when she twirled complemented the blouse, her waist and the festival perfectly. And to top it off her cheeks glowed, not because of rouge or sunburn but because Jack was coming along.

Her heart pitter-pattered like a teenager waiting for her date to prom. She pressed her hands to her cheeks and laughed. This was silly. What thirty-one-year-old woman got all excited about going on a group date with a bunch of her colleagues?

*This one.*

If she played her cards right and she

hadn't read Jack wrong, she might invite him into her bed for a repeat performance of the previous night's activities on the deck. Natalie lifted a tiny bottle of perfume, another item Hallie loaned her, and sprayed on a dash of courage.

"I'm ready." Her eyes widened and her knees shook. Last night had been spontaneous, a product of moonlight and soft kisses. Tonight—holy crap—she had seduction on her mind.

Smoothing her damp hands down the front of her skirt, she checked the fit of the buckle on her sandals and ran out of ways to procrastinate.

A knock on her door made her jump.

*Ready or not, here I come.*

She twisted the handle and flung open the door.

Jack stood in front of her, wearing a crisp white shirt, tailored black trousers and black dress shoes. His shaggy blond hair had been trimmed and he'd shaved. He could have stepped right off the pages of *GQ* magazine.

Natalie pressed a hand to her chest. The man was so handsome, he took her breath away.

His nostrils flared and his eyes darkened. "Hey, beautiful."

The way he said those words made Natalie's knees wobble and her heart pound against her ribs. "Hey, yourself."

"Turn around," he demanded.

She frowned.

He took her hand and twirled her under his arm until she faced away from him. Then he stopped her by placing his hands on her shoulders. "Just as I thought. As pretty from the back as from the front." He moved his hands away.

When Natalie started to turn back around, he said, "Uh-uh. Stay."

She snorted softly. "I'm not a dog."

"Humor me."

Then she felt his fingers against the bare skin of her neck and he draped a silver necklace around her throat, one with a bright red pendent hanging down from the middle. "What's this?"

"Just a little trinket. I couldn't have planned it better. The pendent matches the red in your dress."

He hooked the clasp, his knuckles against the back of her neck sending delicious shivers across her skin, raising gooseflesh.

"You smell good," he whispered the words against her ear and turned her to face him.

Natalie touched the pendent with her fingertips. "You didn't have to bring me a present."

"Yes, I did." He brushed his thumb across her cheek. "A beautiful woman should have beautiful things."

With a shake of her head, she laughed. "You're such a romantic."

"Only when it's warranted."

"Hey, are you two ready?" Hallie passed by in the hallway. "The boat leaves in two minutes."

"Who's staying on board?" Jack asked.

"Steve, Ronnie and their guns." Natalie's lips twisted. Why did their mission have to be so dangerous? All they wanted to do was help save lives. "Will they be okay?"

"They should be." He frowned. "But maybe I should let them use one of my weapons." He grabbed her hand and led her down the hallway to the room he shared with Mac. Without Mac there, they had enough room to stand inside.

The door shut behind Natalie and her breath caught in her throat. They were alone. No one would pass by in the hallway and see them without first opening the door. The perfect opportunity to steal a kiss.

Jack went straight for his closet, pulled out his duffle bag and laid it on his bunk. "I keep a breakdown rifle in my duffle."

"Oh, really?" Disappointment that he didn't seem as eager as she was to pick up where they'd left off the night before shot through her.

Jack started to open the duffle, paused and turned. "You know, we're all alone in here and, no matter how hard I'm trying to be a gentleman, I can't resist."

Her pulse hammered through her veins. "Resist what?"

"This." He pulled her into his arms and crushed her lips with his.

Natalie melted against him, her breasts tingled and her core heated when their bodies pressed together.

"We don't have to go, you know," he suggested, tracing kisses along her jaw.

What she wouldn't give to have the boat to herself, just her and Jack and an entire night lying naked in her bed, making love until the sun came up over the ocean. She sighed. "Unfortunately, we have to. I can't let my team go to town without me. What if something happened to them? I would feel responsible."

Jack kissed her again. "I know. But asking didn't hurt." He pulled several gun parts out of the duffle bag and slipped them together, making a wicked-looking rifle.

Natalie's stomach flipped. She remembered what Mac had said. "Is something like this very expensive?"

He filled a clip full of bullets and nodded. "Yes. I collect guns as a hobby. And since I only have so much room…this one fit the best. Remind me to tell you my life story when we have time. It'll give you a little insight into who I am, and won't take more than fifteen minutes." He winked. "My stories are really kind of repetitive."

Placated by his explanation for the gun, her interest piqued by his promise to tell her his life story, Natalie banished Mac's misgivings about Jack and followed him out of the room and down the hallway to Steve's.

A quick knock and Steve answered. "I was just on my way up to take a turn on the deck and give Ronnie a break." He glanced at the rifle in Jack's hands. "What have you got there?"

"A little extra oomph, in case someone tries to board the *Nightingale* without your permission."

"Sweet." Steve took the gun from Jack. "Wish I had time to practice with it. You sure you don't need it in town tonight?"

Jack grinned. "I'm not sure the locals would like seeing a tourist wielding a high-powered rifle on festival night."

"Definitely not," Natalie agreed and then glanced at Jack. "Are you carrying a gun?"

He nodded and stuck his hand inside his shirt, pulling out a nine-millimeter pistol.

Natalie bit her lip. "You think we'll need it tonight? Maybe we should cancel our trip into Trujillo for the festival."

"The decision's up to you. As big a town as Trujillo is, I figure the guerillas won't attack. Especially during a festival when the town will be full to overflowing with tourists and additional police to help keep the peace."

Natalie chewed on her lower lip, debating whether or not going to the festival was safe. "If we don't go, I know at least one person who will be unhappy."

Steve answered with a grin, "Hallie."

Natalie pushed back her shoulders. "We won't stay long." She touched Jack's arm. "And we have you to protect us."

"Only if we are really good about staying together. I can't be in more than one place at a time."

"We'll have to be clear with the team to stick together." Natalie glanced at Steve. "Are you sure you and Ronnie will be all right out here by yourself?"

"I plan on staying wide awake and watching the water for any craft in our vicinity." He patted the rifle. "And now that I have this, I can take care of anything that comes too close without permission."

Jack's brows puckered. "Yeah, well, don't shoot us when we come back to the boat."

Steve grinned. "I won't."

Natalie led the way to the rear of the boat where Mac, Hallie, Daphne and Dr. Biacowski waited for them to board the dinghy.

"I'm glad you decided to come, Craig," she said.

He shrugged. "I'm feeling so much better, I thought the night out wouldn't hurt."

"Dr. Rhoades and I will take the jet ski," Jack said. "No use overloading the skiff."

"I'd love to ride on the jet ski," Hallie said. "And I'm not wearing a long skirt, like Dr. Rhoades." She stood, waving a hand at her long, slender legs in a short mini skirt.

"Makes sense." Mac held out his hand to Natalie. "Come on, you don't want to get that pretty dress all wet."

Natalie glanced from Jack to Mac and back. Though she wanted to ride with Jack, she didn't want to disappoint Hallie, so she helped Hallie out of the boat. Mac helped her in and they took off.

Had she known Jack would take the jet ski, she might have opted for a shorter skirt. Now she was stuck watching Hallie climb on the back with Jack, wrapping her long, sexy, younger legs around him. A stab of jealousy rocked her more than the boat, and she squeezed her hands into fists to keep from saying or doing something stupid.

Jack wasn't hers to tell whose body he could or couldn't have wrapped around him. They'd had one night of incredibly hot sex. That didn't make him her property or her his.

Rather than watch Hallie laughing out loud as Jack spun the jet ski around and zoomed toward shore, Natalie closed her eyes and held on as they motored over to the dock and tied off.

Not the best start to the evening, but Natalie refused to let it taint her fun. She gave Mac a bright smile as he helped her out of the boat.

The town was lit up and raucous music blared so loudly from the town square, they could hear it all the way out to the docks.

"Come on!" Hallie cried. "Let's party." She grabbed Jack's hand and started to drag him toward the town center.

"Wait," Natalie called out. "We need to establish a few ground rules."

Hallie's face fell. "Really? We're all adults. Don't you think we can use our common sense?"

"Normally, yes." Natalie smiled to soften her words. "With the guerilla faction so close, we need to stick together. Don't wander too far away from the others and stay near the center of town. I don't want anyone kidnapped and dragged off to God knows where." She stared around at the group. "Agreed?"

They all spoke as one, "Agreed."

"We'll leave here at eleven o'clock to head back to the boat."

"Eleven?" Hallie wailed. "The party will just be getting started."

"We all have to get back in the same boat, and I know some of us don't want to stay that long, me included." She glanced around the group. "So, rather than leave at ten, we'll split the distance between ten and twelve and leave at eleven. Sound fair?"

Hallie pouted. "I suppose."

Daphne shrugged. "I'm good with it."

Dr. Biacowski frowned. "I'd rather leave at nine."

"Come on, Craig." Natalie hooked his arm. "We've been working hard. We should stretch our legs and have a little fun. Besides, you owe me a dance."

Natalie shot a glance at Jack as she led Craig into town. Was that a twinge of a frown denting his forehead?

Her smile broadened. Not that she was the type of woman to play games and make a man jealous, but if it did...so be it.

Craig grumbled all the way into the center of town, complaining about the crowd and too many people. The man was an introvert and all the people crammed into the town square made him uncomfortable.

Natalie was surprised he'd volunteered to come in the first place. She wove through the throng until they reached the area where people were dancing in the street. A mariachi band with fiddles, accordions and trumpets perched on a wooden stage in front of an old church.

Women of all shapes and sizes twirled in brightly colored skirts. Men raised their hands and clapped in time to the music.

Natalie led Craig out into the middle of the street and showed him how to do the Salsa-style of dancing, using the most basic steps. After a few minutes, his fierce concentration turned to a tentative smile.

Jack twirled Daphne around, while Mac danced with Hallie. The group was holding to Natalie's words of warning and staying close together.

When the next song started, Mac switched with Craig. For the following five minutes, Natalie danced with the former Army medic, smiling and laughing at something he'd said. The entire time, she could feel Jack's gaze on her and it made her warm inside, knowing he couldn't keep his eyes off her when he had the pretty deckhand, Daphne, to dance with.

As the second song wound to a stop, the group met on the edges of the street to catch their breath.

"Man, I needed this." Hallie fanned herself with her hand. "I call dibs on Jack for the next dance."

The band slipped into a slow dance.

"Sorry." Jack glanced at Hallie. "Next dance? I promised this one to Natalie."

Natalie's cheeks heated as he extended his hand.

Hallie pouted. "As long as I get to dance with you at least once tonight." She winked and grabbed Mac's hand. "Come on, this one is more your speed."

Craig offered his arm to Daphne, and they all blended into the crowd of dancers.

Natalie slipped into Jack's arms, her body

fitting perfectly against his.

He leaned his cheek against her temple and pressed a firm, strong hand low against her back.

Natalie's core sizzled and she wished they were back in the moonlight on the *Nightingale's* deck, naked and making love. Laying her cheek against his chest, she listened to the steady beat of his heart.

"Have I told you how beautiful you are?"

His voice enveloped her like a warm blanket. "Only once. But it wouldn't hurt to repeat yourself. I'm a sucker for flattery." She looked up and fell into his deep blue eyes. "What is it about you that I find so incredibly attractive?"

He didn't smile as she'd intended for him to. Instead, he stopped in the middle of the dance and captured her cheeks between his palms. "I could ask the same." Then he kissed her, drawing her into him with his lips.

They could have been the only two people in Trujillo, or on the planet, for all Natalie could remember.

When he set her away from him, he shook his head. "I don't know what to do with you. I just don't know."

She frowned. "What *should* you do with me?" *Besides make mad, passionate love.* God, had she said that out loud? She held her breath, waiting for his response.

"I want to take you away from here, strip

you naked and make love until the sun sets on the next day and the next."

She gave a shaky laugh and rested her palms on his chest. "What's stopping you?"

He closed his eyes for a moment, then looked at her again, his expression one of regret.

Natalie's heart sank. Not the one reaction she'd been hoping for.

"There is much you don't know about me," he admitted.

"You promised to enlighten me."

"I can't now, but I will soon. There are obstacles that would make being together for the long haul impossible."

Her heart fluttered at the reference to a long-term relationship. She hadn't realized it, but now that she thought about the issue, she wanted to see more of him. When she'd hired him onto the *Nightingale*, she'd gotten the distinct impression he wasn't the kind of deckhand or security guy who'd stay around. He had that air of a drifter, someone who didn't have roots to hold him down. She'd hired him anyway.

"I won't always be around," he confirmed. "Natalie, you need a man who can always be there for you."

She snorted. "What did I tell you last night? You can't bank on tomorrow. This life has no guarantees."

"And you have to grab for whatever

happiness you can find, when you find it." He sighed. "That's why I grabbed you last night, and why I want you now. You're an amazing woman. If I was anyone but who I am, I'd want to stay and get to know you better, make love to you every day for the rest our lives together. But I can't, and I won't lead you on."

"I knew when I hired you that you wouldn't be around forever. I took my chances then, I'm willing to take them now." She smoothed a hand over his muscled back. "Whatever you have to give, I'll take, and give back to you in return."

"You don't understand." He pulled her against him and rocked to the slow, sad song. "I've kept secrets from you."

Natalie rested her cheek against his chest. "Unless you're married, a serial killer or a drug dealer, I don't care."

He stopped again and lifted her face to stare down into her eyes. "You're a remarkable woman, Natalie Rhoades. I won't hurt you. This, what we have between us, ends now before it goes too far."

Her heart clenched. "We passed the point of too far last night. You end it now and you hurt me. I know you're not sticking around. I accept that. What you're saying is you aren't giving me a choice to continue with what we have until you leave. You're making that choice for me."

"I didn't want to hurt you."

"Damn you, Jack. I'm a big girl. I make my own decisions and live with the consequences. If you don't want to see me anymore, just say so." She pushed against his chest and backed away, bumping into another pair of dancers. "Excuse me. I need to take a break." She turned and ran to the edge of the crowd before she stopped. "I will not cry," she said. "I will not cry."

"Hey, Dr. Rhoades," Hallie's voice sounded behind her and a gentle hand touched her shoulder. "Are you okay?"

Natalie nodded. "I'm fine."

"Fine fine? Or not so fine fine?" Hallie laughed then her face grew more serious. "You and Jack have a fight?"

"No." So she'd been obvious. *Great.* "He's just our security guy."

"Uh-huh." Her hands fisted on her hips. "I see the way you look at him."

Natalie sighed. "The feeling only goes one way, though."

"No, ma'am. I've also seen the way he looks at you. The man's got it bad for our pretty doctor."

"No, you have it all wrong. He just ended it before anything had a chance to start." Natalie laughed, choking down a sob.

"Oh, sweetheart, that's man-speak for I want to stop before I hurt myself." Hallie slipped an arm around Natalie's waist and hugged her.

Natalie's gaze followed Jack's confident figure as he wove his way through the throng to the opposite side of the street and made a broad sweep around the town square. "You think so?"

"Absolutely. Look at him." Hallie nodded toward the sexy man. All the ladies' heads turned as he passed. "He's running away."

"From me. As fast as he can go."

"No, he's running away from his feelings *for* you." Hallie shook her head. "Men are so predictable. They're rather face a dozen enemy soldiers than their own feelings."

"How do you know so much about men?" Natalie turned to the younger woman.

Her lips twisted and her eyes glazed. "Let's just say I've had my share of bad relationships."

"Thanks." Natalie leaned against Hallie. "For keeping me balanced."

"Sure." Hallie glanced toward Craig who was dancing with Daphne and Mac with a heavyset female tourist. "Should I end Craig and Mac's torture so we can head back to the *Nightingale*? They didn't want to dance in the first place."

Natalie shook her head. "I'm content to people-watch for a little while, and getting some exercise won't hurt Craig and Mac. You came to dance."

A handsome young Honduran man held

out his hand to Natalie and, in Spanish, asked her to dance.

Smiling, she shook her head. "Gracias, no." Natalie turned to Hallie and gave her a shove forward.

The man offered his hand to Hallie.

"Second choice? Ah, who cares? *Gracias.*" Hallie grinned and placed her hand in his. He whisked her out into the middle of the dancers and spun her around again and again. She laughed out loud, her smile outshining the stars.

Natalie couldn't help smiling with her, before searching the crowd for Jack. Several minutes passed before she spotted him. When she did, she frowned. He stood at a street corner talking to another man with equally broad shoulders and tanned skin.

Who did he know in Trujillo?

Natalie stepped into the crowd, headed toward him.

Jack would have followed Natalie when she'd walked away, but Gator had news he wanted to share in person. Keeping a close eye on Natalie, Hallie, Daphne and the guys, he made his way through the crowd to the corner of a small church. "Whatcha got?"

"The drone picked up movement outside of Trujillo on a less-traveled dirt road that leads into the interior."

"What kind of movement?" He tensed,

knowing this was what they'd waited for.

"Two trucks that appear to be loaded with men."

"Road workers or guerillas?"

"Men carrying weapons."

Jack's jaw hardened, his gaze slipping to Natalie. "Headed this way?"

"Yes."

Jack faced Gator. "When?"

"Just before sunset."

"Great." The guerillas could be positioning themselves on the outskirts of Trujillo, ready to stage an attack. Jack's gaze returned to Natalie as she worked her way through the crowd toward him, a frown marring her pretty forehead. "I'll gather the medical team and herd them back toward the dock. I don't want them caught in the crossfire. A moment ago, I spotted Dustman and Irish in the crowd."

"Good. I have men stationed at as many of the town entry points as we could find. They are well hidden. The trouble is, we don't know if some of the guerillas are already here, among the festival goers."

Jack stared at the crowd, his senses on overload.

A dark-haired man captured Natalie in his arms and swung her around to the beat of the music.

*Damn.* Jack took a step forward and stopped when Natalie laughed and ducked under the man's arm, leaving him dancing by himself in the middle of the street.

"Here comes your doctor lady." Gator nodded toward Natalie. "You'd better go."

Jack pushed through the colorfully dressed women and men, his locked gaze on Natalie, while he watched in his peripheral vision for signs of guerillas in disguise.

"Who were you talking to?" Natalie asked when she reached him.

"Someone I know," Jack responded. "Where are the others? We need to start back to the boat."

"Why?"

"There might be trouble, and I don't want you and the team caught in the middle of it."

Natalie spun. "They were dancing on the other side of the square." She pointed toward Craig and Daphne. "There's Dr. Biacowski and Daphne. Mac's dancing with a woman close to them and Hallie…" She frowned, her head moving as she scanned the crowd.

"Where's Hallie?" Jack grabbed Natalie's hand and shoved his way through.

"She was dancing with a man there in the middle just a second ago. I kept an eye on them until…"

"I saw her, too, just a minute ago."

"She can't have gone far." Natalie took the lead, stopping when she reached Mac, Craig and Daphne. "Have you seen Hallie?"

"I thought she was with you." Mac thanked the woman he'd been dancing with and craned his neck, searching for the missing member of their party. "She was right next to us for a while."

Jack had a sinking feeling. "Wait here." He stepped away from the medical team and scanned the crowd, locating Dustman as the closest of his SEAL team. Touching his finger to the communication device in his ear, he said, "Dustman, I could use your assistance."

"What's wrong?" Gator cut in.

"Missing one member of the medical team. The blonde, Hallie Kristofer," Jack responded. "I need one or two men to escort the remaining medical staff to the boat."

"You heard the man," Gator said to the rest of the team online. "Watch out for the young blond woman. Dustman and Irish, help out Fish."

Dustman straightened and powered his way through the throng toward Jack. From another direction, Irish appeared out of a shadowy corner and swam through the merrymakers.

When they converged on Jack, he turned to the four members of the floating doctor team.

Jack introduced the two men. "No time to explain. These two men are my friends, Dustin and Declan. They will escort you back to the boat."

Natalie crossed her arms. "Sorry, but I'm not going anywhere without Hallie. We need to be looking for her."

"Agreed." Mac glared. "Especially since I have no idea who these goons are."

Irish grinned and Dustman gave Mac the stink-eye.

If the situation had been different, Jack would have laughed at Mac's description of his SEAL brothers. "Okay, the short explanation is this: Dustin and Declan are SEALs, here on a mission to find and rescue several men who have been taken captive by the Castillo Commandos. They're holding them hostage in some undisclosed location we have yet to locate. I—we had reason to believe your team had become the next target of the guerillas."

"We?" Natalie bit into the word like a pit bull into a bone. "Are you with them?" She turned her stare toward Dustman and Irish. "Is he one of you? A SEAL?"

Dustman shot a glance at Jack.

Irish grinned. "Yes, ma'am."

Frowning, Natalie turned to Jack. "That's the secret you were keeping?"

Hearing the condemnation in her tone, Jack nodded.

Natalie's lips thinned. "It doesn't matter now. The important thing is to find Hallie." She turned to the others. "Work in pairs. Don't lose track of your buddy and stay in sight of the town square."

"Whoa! Whoa! Whoa!" Jack held up his hands. "You are not going to find her yourselves. Dr. Rhoades, you and your team are in danger. Go back to the *Nightingale* and stay put until you hear from me."

"You might be a SEAL, but you're not my boss, and I don't take orders from you. One of my team is missing. I'm not returning to my boat until we find her."

Dustman and Irish's eyes widened and they glanced at Jack.

"She's right, you know," Dustman commented.

"I could throw her over my shoulder and carry her back to the dock." Irish rubbed his hands together.

Mac stepped between Jack and Natalie. "I'll stay with Dr. Rhoades. The more people looking for Hallie, the faster we find her."

"What if the guerillas head out to the boat?" Daphne waved an arm toward the bay. "Steve and the skipper are alone out there."

Natalie nodded. "And we're wasting time arguing about it." She hooked Mac's arm. "I'm with Mac. You SEALs can escort Daphne and Dr. Biacowski back to the dock, if you want to be helpful. They can help Steve and the skipper defend the boat."

"We can't leave without Hallie," Daphne said.

"Steve and Ronnie need you. We'll find

Hallie." Natalie gave Daphne and the other doctor a pointed stare. "Please. Go."

The two weren't happy, but they let Irish and Dustman march them back to the dock.

Natalie turned away from Jack. "Come on, it's already been too long since we last saw her."

"I'm coming with you," Jack said.

"Do what you want." Natalie didn't look backward, only marched forward, her head swiveling right and left, her brows furrowed, her face pale.

Jack could kick himself for taking his focus off the medical team for even a moment. If he hadn't been so obsessed with their leader, he would have been more alert to signs of trouble.

"The last time I saw Hallie, she was right about here, dancing with who I thought was a nice-looking Honduran local." Natalie stopped and stared across the crowded square.

Jack searched the tops of the heads of the persons dancing to the lively music. Most had dark hair. The few that didn't were gray-haired tourists. He turned, searching for the closest escape route from the town square—one a guerilla would use to get Hallie away from the rest fairly quickly. The street behind him was narrow and shadowed. "Stay here, I'm checking out the end of this street."

"We're going, too," Natalie said.

"And if she turns up in the town square, you'll miss her." Jack shook his head. "I'm not telling you to stay. I'm asking you to be here in case she shows up."

Natalie bit down on her lip. "I don't like just standing still."

"Then move around, but not far and not away from the crowd. Stay together, and you shouldn't be accosted. "I'll be right back."

Jack turned and ran to the end of the street. Looking back over his shoulder, he spotted Natalie and Mac standing on their toes, searching the crowd for Hallie.

The narrow alley ended at a T-intersection. When he turned left, nothing moved. Swinging his glance to the right, he thought he saw someone slip up the alley headed back toward the crowded square. Jack hesitated and glanced toward the square.

Natalie and Mac still stood at the opposite end of the alley by themselves. They'd be fine for just a minute while he checked out the movement.

Racing to the next cross street, Jack turned. Again, a shadowy figure disappeared around the corner, headed back the direction where the doctor and medic had been standing but on a different street.

His heart thrumming against his chest, Jack ran to the end of the alley and out. He turned right, looking across to where he started. He'd been away for maybe a minute, and both Natalie and Mac were gone.

# Chapter Seven

When she saw Jack disappear around the corner at the end of the alley, Natalie's pulse rocketed. He was alone. If the guerillas were out there and they knew he was a SEAL, he could be easily outnumbered. "We should follow him."

"No," Mac said. "Keep looking for Hallie."

Natalie alternated between searching the crowd for Hallie and watching for Jack to reappear. "What if Jack gets in trouble?"

"The man's a SEAL. Which explains his access to expensive weapons." Mac's hand shot out and clutched her arm. "I saw blond hair."

Natalie swung around and stared in the direction Mac was looking.

He grabbed her hand. "Come on."

Natalie had no choice but to follow or be dragged behind him. "What about Jack?"

"He'll be okay. If we wait for him to come back, she could be gone," Mac shouted over his shoulder, running so fast Natalie had trouble matching his pace.

"There!" Mac pointed toward a street that led off the square. "Someone took her down that street."

Natalie had seen the flash of blond hair, and her blood raced through her veins. "Hallie!" She dropped Mac's hand, dodged a drunk and ran as fast as she could toward the street. When she reached it, she stopped, her lungs screaming for air. "Where did they go?" she asked.

Mac kept running. "I don't know, but we can't lose her now."

"Mac, wait!" Natalie sucked in a deep breath and tore out after him.

He reached the end of the street before her. It T-junctioned, forcing them to turn right or left, or run straight into the jungle.

Natalie heard a loud crack and a deep grunt as she neared the corner. She was running too fast to come to a quick stop. Mac slumped to the ground in front of her, his body a large obstacle directly in her path.

She planted her feet in the ground, but the gravel slipped beneath her sandals. Her momentum propelled her forward and she toppled over Mac's inert form, landing with a crash, her head smacking the hard ground.

What little light was left in the dark alley snuffed out.

Jack spoke into his communication device. "I've lost Natalie and Mac."

"What the hell?" Gator said. "I leave you with the easy job, and you lose two more?"

"Cut the crap. I'm serious," Jack spun in

a three-sixty, desperately searching for Natalie. "I don't see them anywhere."

"Holy shit, there's the blonde," Gator said. "I found the blonde."

"Good, now find Natalie and Mac." Jack ran to the next street and peered into the unlit corners. No Natalie. Blood pounding, he ran to the next and the next until he reached the big church at the end of the square.

Gator emerged from the street leading to the right of the church with an arm around Hallie's waist.

The woman's hair was disheveled and her makeup smeared, but she was alive, a bruise on one cheek.

"What happened?" Jack demanded.

"The guy I was dancing with maneuvered me over to the side of the crowd and then jerked me onto a dark street. There were two other men who grabbed me and...and." She swallowed hard on a sob and continued. "They dragged me out into the jungle saying something about a doctor. When I told them I wasn't a doctor, they stopped and turned back to the crowd." Hallie's eyes widened and she looked around Jack. "Where's Dr. Rhoades?"

Jack's jaw hardened. "Missing."

"Oh, my god. They have her?" Hallie burst into tears and flung herself on Gator's shoulder.

"Can you get her to the *Nightingale*? If you need it, my jet ski is moored at the dock."

"I'll get her there," Gator assured him.

"Gator, we found one of the medical team," a voice said into Jack's ear.

Gator handed Hallie to Jack and cupped a hand over his ear to block out the noise from the band. "Where?"

"At the edge of the jungle on the west side of town. He's unconscious, but alive."

*He?* Jack pushed Hallie back into Gator's arms and ran down a street to the edge of town. The jungle crept up to the dirt street that bordered Trujillo. He looked both ways and saw a couple of dark figures standing around a lump on the ground and trotted over to the men.

Mac pushed to a sitting position, holding his head in his hands. "Where's Doc Rhoades?"

"We were hoping you could tell us," Jack said, as he scanned the area.

"Damn. All I know is I saw someone leading a blonde down this alley. I ran after them and when I got to this point, everything went black."

Swede stepped forward. "Big Bird found a trail through the jungle. He and Tuck are on it now."

"Speaking of that trail," Tuck's voice said into the headset in Jack's ear. "It leads to another dirt road. Fresh tire tracks were present."

Jack stared at Mac, a sick feeling grabbing

his stomach. "It appears the boss has been kidnapped."

"Fuck." Mac pressed a hand to his head and came back with blood. "Fuck, that hurt." He glanced up at Jack. "You have to find her."

Jack nodded, his heart sore. He'd let her down, but he'd make it up to her. "We will find her."

Natalie came to in pitch blackness. A musty cloth covered her face, and the surface she lay on rocked and rumbled like the bed of a large truck. The smell of dust and vehicle fumes teased her nose. She assumed she'd been loaded into the back of a truck and was being transported. Where they were going, she had no clue. She coughed and tried to move her hands, but they were tied behind her back with what felt like rough hemp rope.

Basically blind and incapacitated, she could either lie there and await her fate or try to escape her confines. Natalie pulled her knees against her chest and tried to roll up onto them. The truck hit a big bump and she sprawled out over the metal floor with a frustrated grunt. After several attempts, she finally maneuvered her way into a kneeling position, but she couldn't get the bag off her head. She assumed it was still dark outside because no light came up through the bottom edges of the bag.

Trying everything she could think of, she couldn't shake the bag from her head. Eventually, the truck jerked to a stop. Muffled shouts erupted outside the vehicle. The words sounded like Spanish, but were spoken so fast, Natalie couldn't translate.

Metal clanked against metal like a tailgate dropping. Someone climbed up in the back of the truck beside her, grabbed her arm and dragged her to the edge.

Two sets of meaty hands hooked her beneath the arms and pulled her out of the truck to stand in slippery mud that oozed around the edges of her sandals, covering her feet. The air smelled of fresh rain and decaying vegetation, thick and humid like in the deepest jungle.

Gray light shone from the bottom of her hood. Natalie wondered how long she'd been out. Was it morning or the next evening?

A gruff voice spoke, "*Traerla!*"

The big hands half-guided and half-dragged her several yards. Natalie bumped into what she assumed was a doorway, and she was shoved into a building. The first thing that hit her was the smell of vomit and feces. Feet shuffled nearby and someone coughed, a weak, pathetic sound.

Straining to see what little she could, Natalie tried to keep calm and figure a way out of the mess she'd landed in.

Her escort ripped the hood from her

head, and she blinked in the sudden light from a camping lantern set on a nearby table. Two women stood to one side, their hair pulled back in long braids. They wore long skirts with aprons tied over them and stared, wide-eyed.

The men on either side of her could have been bouncers at any Honduran nightclub. Their more likely occupation was terrorists belonging to the Castillo Commandos Jack had talked about.

Natalie shivered at the sight of the military rifles they carried slung over their shoulders and the pistols they held pointed at her.

The man on her left jerked his pistol, motioning her forward.

One wall of the cramped room was completely filled by a small bed. A man lay in it, his face pale, sallow and covered with perspiration. Buried in roughly woven blankets, he shook so hard, the wooden headboard rattled against the wall.

The doctor in Natalie ticked off the symptoms. Chills, vomiting and diarrhea. Symptoms that could belong to a number of diseases or sicknesses.

The man beside her spoke rapid-fire Spanish, once again too fast for Natalie to translate. She did pick up on a name. Ramon.

The man in the bed opened his eyes and turned his head toward her. He lifted his hand

and motioned her closer.

Natalie inched forward.

When she stood beside the bed, the man closed his eyes again and spoke in halting English. "I am sick."

"Yes, it appears you are," she said, without leaning down to examine him or to touch him in anyway.

"What is it? Can you cure me?"

He opened his eyes again, and she could see that they were bloodshot, the whites a dull yellow.

*Possibly malaria.* Natalie shrugged. "Not without diagnostic tools and medication. And of course, I can't help you at all with my hands tied."

Ramon mumbled something.

One of the goons untied her wrists while the other left and came back a moment later with a large wooden box. He dumped it on the floor and flung open the lid. Inside was a jumble of medical equipment, medications and a stethoscope lying in haphazard array as if they'd been thrown in.

After rubbing her hands together to regain dexterity, Natalie lifted one of the bottles of medicine and noted the date and manufacturer. This was one of the medicines she'd delivered to the hospital in Trujillo. Keeping her expression neutral, she hoped none of the staff members had been harmed in the theft of the items.

One of the items in the box was a microscope with several glass slides, some of which were broken. With the microscope were several of the Rapid Diagnostic Test cards she'd left with the doctor.

She pulled the microscope, slides and RDTs out carefully and laid them on a small wooden table in the corner. Then she removed the stethoscope and a bottle of rubbing alcohol and quickly cleaned the earpieces and the chest piece. She examined the patient and added respiratory difficulties to the list of symptoms. Leaning back, she stared down into the man's eyes. "Without a blood workup, I can't tell you what you have. I need a blood sample. And even then, I might not have everything here I need."

The man in the bed reached up and grabbed the necklace around her neck and pulled her down to where they were eye to eye. "If you don't help me, I will have my men kill you." He let go and slumped against the mattress.

Natalie jerked back, her heart thumping. "I'll do what I can, with what I have." She touched a hand to the necklace Jack had given her, thankful the chain hadn't broken. It gave her a small sense of comfort she sorely needed.

Even if she managed to escape from her captors, she had no idea where she was. Because they had traveled all night, they were quite a distance from Trujillo. How would Jack and his Navy SEAL brothers find her in the jungles of Honduras?

Heart heavy, she reached for a handful of Rapid Diagnostic Test cards and a scalpel. When she hovered over Roman, holding the scalpel, the two goons who'd shoved her through the door rushed forward, pointing their guns at her head.

She pushed them aside. "Look, I can't work with guns in my face. Either shoot me or let me do my job."

Ramon spoke to them, muttering low in a guttural Spanish.

They backed away and Natalie went to work. Given the symptoms and the damp conditions outside, she started with the easiest and most likely test first that only needed a drop of blood. Others required stool samples or more extensive blood testing of which she doubted she had the necessary stains to make an accurate test.

She poked the tip of Ramon's finger and squeezed it until a drop of blood balled up on the tip. He was so weak, he didn't complain or jerk his hand away. Grabbing the RDT card, she pressed the droplet in the appropriate place and waited the required amount of time.

As she suspected, the man tested positive for malaria. She riffled through the box for the medication he'd need to cure the illness. Thankfully, there were several bottles of

Quinine pills. She shook one of the pills out into her hand and looked to the women. "He'll need a drink of water. *Agua*." Natalie motioned with her hands, indicating a drink.

One of the women turned and poured water from a bucket into a cup and carried it to Natalie.

She stared at the murky water and felt her stomach jump then shook her head. She asked for bottled water or bottled drinks of any kind.

The woman hurried from the hut and returned with a bottled fruit drink.

While Natalie helped the man to lean upright enough to swallow the pill with a sip of the drink, she used her primitive Spanish, instructing the women to boil their drinking and cooking water before consuming it to kill the parasites and germs.

When Ramon was settled back against the bed, she glanced at the others in the room. They didn't appear to be affected by malaria at that time.

In her slow Spanish, she asked the ladies, "Is there standing water near the camp?"

One nodded and answered in Spanish, "Yes. It rains here."

"Standing water allows mosquitoes to breed. If Ramon has Malaria, others in your camp will have it." She was thankful she'd had her vaccination against the debilitating disease.

"Yes, yes." The shorter woman hurried

to the door and motioned for Natalie to follow.

When she stepped that way, carrying the bottle of pills and the fruit drink, she was blocked by one of the big, burly men stepping into her path.

"Ramon, *por favor*," the woman pleaded.

The man in the bed spoke to the guards in Spanish, "Follow her."

Natalie trailed the woman through the mud to another shack, built of a variety of bits of wood and tin.

Once inside, the native lit a candle and carried it to a pallet on the floor. A small girl lay in a blanket, her face beaded in sweat. Her little body shook and she moaned.

Natalie cut one of the pills in quarters and helped the little one to swallow it with more of the fruit drink she'd carried from Ramon's hut. She left several of the pills with the woman with clear instructions on how to administer them. "Are there others?" she asked.

The woman looked to the men guarding Natalie and nodded. She spoke to the men in her Spanish so rapid, Natalie couldn't keep up. She caught every other word, especially when the woman said Americano.

Had they brought her to the camp where they kept the hostages being held for ransom?

The guards shook their heads.

The woman frowned and more or less

138

scolded them.

Finally, they sighed and motioned for Natalie to follow.

Back out in the mud, she trudged to yet another hut. This one was guarded by a man at the front and another at the rear, both carrying military-style rifles. They moved aside when one of Natalie's guards spoke.

Inside, the room was dark. She didn't have the benefit of a candle or lantern. She stood in the darkness, letting her eyes adjust to the little bit of light streaming through the open door.

A moan sounded from the floor to the right.

"I'm Dr. Natalie Rhoades. Are you Americans?"

She waited only a moment before two voices sounded at once. "Yes."

# Chapter Eight

The sun was low on the horizon when Jack checked his equipment for the fifth time. He had his rifle slung over his shoulder, a nine-millimeter tucked into a holster and another tucked into his boot. Two Black Hawk helicopters soared over the Honduran jungle, headed to the coordinates indicated by the GPS tracking device located in the necklace he'd given Natalie before they'd gone to the festival.

He prayed the guerillas hadn't injured her and that she hadn't been separated from the device in transit. Otherwise, they could be way off course and miss their target all together.

"Five minutes," Gator called out.

Closest to the open door, Jack grabbed the rope and held on. The helicopters flew low, practically skimming the canopy so the enemy wouldn't hear their approach. They would drop to ground a couple miles from the camp and hike in from there.

"Ready?" Gator said.

Jack's pulse jumped and then settled. Although, they trained for this type of operation so many times he wasn't nervous, he couldn't stop worrying about Natalie. If they didn't get in and find her first, they risked her being used as a human shield or a bargaining chip for the guerillas to buy their way out of the corner the SEALs would force them into.

"Go!"

Jack tossed the end of the rope out of the helicopter, grabbed it with his gloved hands and fast-roped down into the trees. As soon as his feet hit the ground, he moved out of the way to avoid being hit by the next SEAL coming down. Once everyone was accounted for, they moved out swiftly with Jack taking point.

He carried the handheld tracking device and took the most direct route through the jungle to get to the guerilla camp.

Thirty minutes later, he slowed. Through the trees and brush, he spotted a wisp of smoke. He motioned for the others to spread out. As quiet as big cats stalking their prey, the SEALs moved in.

One by one, they reported their sightings of the numbers and locations of the armed guerillas.

No one had yet to report seeing Dr. Rhoades or the wealthy hostages.

Jack noted one hut had a guard at the front and the rear.

Gator slipped up beside him and he pointed to the hut. "That has to be where they keep the hostages." He spoke into his headset. "Irish, Swede, take the guards on the hut at the far end of the camp." They gave the two SEALs time to work their way around the camp, swinging wide to avoid detection. When they reported that they were in place, Gator gave the go-ahead and the SEAL team moved in.

They neared the edges of the camp, and the door to the hut containing the hostages opened and two big guerillas exited followed by Natalie. They flanked her, marching her to another hut.

Jack's pulse jumped and he almost leaped out of position to go after her. Gator's hand on his arm brought him back to reason.

"We'll take the hut she goes into," Gator whispered.

All three entered the building in the middle of the camp. It was the largest and of the best construction. "Fuck," Jack muttered. "Wanna bet they're taking her in to see Ramon Villarreal?"

Gator nodded. "We can't wait until she comes out. That might not happen anytime soon, and the longer we wait, the higher risk of someone stumbling upon one of us."

Jack knew he was right, but how was he getting Natalie out of the hut in which the leader of the Castillo Commandos lived without harming her?

Gator spoke softly into his microphone. "Let's rock this joint."

Darkness settled on the camp sooner than above the jungle's canopy. Like lions in the night, the SEAL team stole into camp and picked off the perimeter guards. No shots were fired and no alarm went up. Irish dispatched the guard on the rear of the hostage building, and Swede took out the one in the front by making a slight noise that drew him to the side.

Because the camp had no electricity, the SEALs had the advantage with their night vision goggles. They could see the enemy in the dark.

Once they had the night shift accounted for, Dustman set charges on the trucks. When he was ready, he spoke into the radio. "Get ready for fireworks."

Jack and Gator covered their ears and slipped their NVGs up.

A loud bang shook the ground beneath them. Men tumbled out of the huts, shouting and firing weapons into the air. When the ensuing fire reached the gasoline in the truck tanks, a louder and more impressive explosion lit up the darkness.

The SEALs moved in.

Big Bird, their best sniper, set up shop on a clear corner of camp and picked off those guerillas carrying guns first.

In all the confusion, Jack, Gator and Dustman kicked open the door to the leader's hut. Jack was first through, diving in to the right. Gator covered, shooting one of the big guys who'd escorted Dr. Rhoades inside. Two women cowered in a corner.

The other guard who'd led Natalie into the hut pulled her in front of him and held his gun to her head.

Jack tensed, sweat breaking out at what he saw.

Gator aimed his weapon at the guard's head and spoke to him in Spanish, "Let her go, or I'll kill you."

"I'll kill her first," he replied.

"I will count to three. If you don't let her go by then, you're a dead man."

The guard's eyes narrowed.

"*Uno.*"

Jack studied the angle and distance he was from Natalie's captor. He could kill the man before he had a chance to pull the trigger. He was an excellent shot at close range and so was Gator. But did he want to risk hitting Natalie?

"*Dos,*" Gator said, his voice low and dangerous.

Jack aimed carefully and fired. The shot rang out and the man holding Natalie jerked, staggered backward, then crumpled to the floor, his gun dropping to the dirt.

Gator glared at Jack, lowering his weapon several inches.

He jumped to his feet. "Sorry, you were taking too long."

Natalie sagged, her entire body trembling. "Oh, Jack." She fell into his arms and wrapped her arms around his waist. "I didn't think you'd find me."

"I'd search to the end of the earth to find you," he whispered as he smelled her familiar scent.

Gator snorted and pointed his gun at the man in the bed who'd leaned over reaching for the weapon on the floor. "Touch it and I'll kill you."

"Ramon Villarreal?" Jack asked.

The man in the bed appeared weak and sickly. But he glared at Jack, refusing to speak.

Natalie answered for him. "Yes. He's Ramon." She touched the necklace around her neck. "He threatened to kill me if I didn't cure him."

"What's he got?"

"Malaria. As do his hostages. The sooner we get them to a medical facility, the better." Still holding him around the middle, she leaned back and looked up into his eyes. "I don't suppose you have transportation?"

He kissed her lips and grinned. "As a matter of fact, we do."

Already they could hear the sound of a helicopter landing in the small clearing beside the camp.

In minutes, they had the hostages, loaded into one helicopter and Ramon and the little girl loaded into the other. The child and

Ramon would be flown to the Honduran capital where they would receive medical care.

"The team will mop up and wait for the Honduran National Army to come collect the guerillas," Gator assured her.

Natalie and Jack rode with the hostages and assisted with their medical needs, watching over them until they reached the U.S.S. *Mercy*. The large hospital ship had been sailing off the coast of Honduras, headed for a mission in Argentina.

Natalie handed off the patients to the doctors on board the medical ship and endured being examined for any lasting effects of being knocked unconscious. When she got the all-clear, she begged a shower and clean scrubs and shower shoes from the medical staff.

Clean of all the mud and germs acquired at the guerilla camp, she craved wide-open spaces and fresh air. And she got it out on the deck. Jack stood by her from the time he found her in Ramon's hut to the time she stepped into the shower, promising he'd be there when she got out. On board the ship, she knew she was safe, but deep down, she worried if she turned away for too long, Jack would disappear out of her life for good.

She knew the fear was stupid. Jack was a Navy SEAL. He was going back to his job wherever that might take him next. He might never have a need to return to Central

146

America. Natalie had her floating doctor boat and the responsibility of keeping it going. For the first time in the two years she'd lived on board, she wished for other options to look forward to.

Once the helicopter had been refueled, they were flown back to Trujillo where they were met by an original crew member of the borrowed luxury yacht. He ferried Natalie and Jack back to the *Nightingale*, promising to pick up Jack the next day.

Exhausted from her ordeal with the Commandos, Natalie wanted nothing more than to crawl into bed and sleep for twenty-four hours. She couldn't. Jack would be gone the next day and she wanted to spend every minute with him until he left.

Her crew met her on deck when she returned.

Hallie flung her arms around her, crying tears of joy. "I'm so glad they found you."

Mac hugged her, too. He had a bandaged knot on his head where he'd been hit. When she tried to examine it, he held up his hands. "Dr. Biacowski checked me over. I'll live." He smiled. "And thanks to Jack and his team of SEALS, so will you." He hugged her, his eyes suspiciously moist. "Welcome back."

After she'd greeted each member individually, she held up her hands. "If you all will excuse me, I want to spend the next twenty-four hours in my own bed."

Hallie gave her sly smile. "Alone?"

Natalie's cheeks heated. "I hope not."

Behind her, Jack answered. "No, she will not be alone. As her personal security guard, I'll make sure she is safe from guerillas and pirates." He took her hand and led her into her stateroom, closing the door with a clunk.

"You don't have to go back to your team?" A quiver started low in her belly.

"Skipper passed on the word the team has the rest of the week off for R&R aboard the *Pegasus*, courtesy of William Bentley, the hostage you treated for malaria. The boat's his."

"A week?" Her pulse racing, Natalie gripped the hem of her scrub shirt and yanked it up over her head. She hadn't had a clean bra to wear beneath it so she'd gone without, condemning the clothes she'd worn in the guerilla camp to the trash. She slipped out of the bottoms and stood before him naked. "Are you joining your brothers on board the *Pegasus* anytime soon?"

Jack laughed and hugged her naked body to him. "Are you kidding me? Not until I absolutely have to."

Natalie helped him pull off the T-shirt and sweatpants the personnel of the medical ship provided him. When he was naked, he pulled her into his arms and held her for a long time, a hand caressing her skin.

Then he pushed her to arm's length, his

expression intense. "Natalie, we've only
known each other a short time."

She smiled and brushed her hand along
the side of his face, loving how rough it was,
trying to brace herself for the words he would
surely say next. He'd want this to be a one-
time deal. Seeing her after he left would be
impossible. They each had their jobs, and
their work was not even in the same country.
Her chest tightened and her eyes burned.
"Yes, Jack?" She looked up and forced a smile
to her lips.

Wincing, he shook his head. "I know I
should say this week will be all we have
together, but I just can't."

Natalie's heart lightened slightly. She
swallowed hard on the lump forming in her
throat. "Go on."

"I don't know how you feel, but I don't
want what we have to end."

"Neither do I. But how can we see each
other if we're not even in the same
geographical area?"

Jack's hand slipped over her shoulder and
down her arm, coming up to cup her breast.
"I don't know, but can we leave it open? I
want to see you again."

She traced the line of his collarbone with
her finger, dragged it down to one of his hard
brown nipples and tweaked it. "I could stand
to take a vacation, at least once a year.
Perhaps we could restock in Virginia? Maybe

even provide services to low-income Americans. I could check into that possibility."

"And I love the tropics. I could spend my vacation helping out on the *Nightingale*." Jack bent, scooped her up into arms and carried her to the bed. He laid her down and stretched out beside her, flashing her a wide grin. "Hell, we haven't even had time to get to know each other. Let's give it a week. If we haven't killed each other, we'll work things out."

"What do you want to know about me?"

"I want to know about the rose tattoo on your ass."

She smiled as she ran her hands up his muscled arms. "Freshman year of college. It was my way of stretching my wings and rebelling against my parent's tyranny. What about the eagle across your shoulder?"

"I got that one after a buddy of mine was killed on a mission." Jack slipped lower down her body and tongued the tip of one breast. "You really are beautiful, inside and out."

He trailed more kissed across her chest to the other breast and sucked it into his mouth, pulling hard. Shifting ever lower, he took his time making it all the way down to the juncture of her thighs. When he parted her folds, she arched her back, digging both heels into the mattress. "Please," she begged.

He tongued her, setting the tightly

packed bundle of nerves on fire.

Natalie moaned. She didn't care if anyone outside her room heard her.

He sucked her clit into his mouth and pulled gently at the same time he slipped a finger into her channel.

Natalie came apart, her senses shattering into a million shivering pieces.

When she could remember to breathe again, she pulled him up her body by a gentle hold on his ears.

"You make me remember I'm female, alive and on fire with passion." She'd pushed the sad memories to the back of her mind to make room for the good ones she'd create with Jack. Happier than she'd been in a very long time, she kissed him. "Make love to me, frogman."

Jack didn't argue. He settled his big body between her legs and slid inside her in one long, beautiful stroke, filling her completely—body and soul.

That night and the subsequent nights in that magical week, he proved he could take orders from her, when they suited him, and she was totally satisfied with his performance.

How they would continue their long-distance relationship would prove a challenge. Natalie vowed to meet the challenge willingly with a heart full of hope and a man who made her heart sing again.

*THE END*

# About the Author

ELLE JAMES also writing as MYLA JACKSON is an award-winning author of books including cowboys, intrigues and paranormal adventures that keep her readers on the edges of their seats. With over seventy works in a variety of sub-genres and lengths she's published with Harlequin, Samhain, Elloras' Cave, Kensington, Cleis Press, and Avon. When she's not at her computer, she's traveling, snow-skiing, boating, or riding her ATV, dreaming up new stories. Learn more about Elle James at www.ellejames.com

Or visit her alter-ego Myla Jackson at mylajackson.com

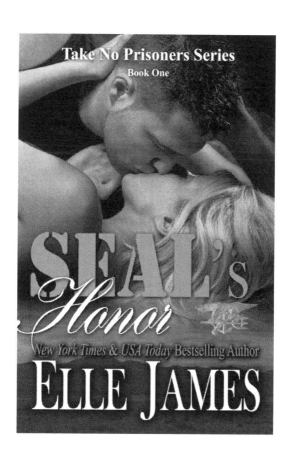

Take No Prisoners Series
Book One

# SEAL's Honor

New York Times & USA Today Bestselling Author

# ELLE JAMES

# SEAL's Honor

## Take No Prisoners Series

© *Elle James*

# Chapter One

Reed Tucker, Tuck to his buddies, tugged at the tie on his U.S. Navy service dress blue uniform, and his gut knotted as he entered the rehabilitation center of the National Naval Medical Center in Bethesda, Maryland.

He'd never run from anything, not a machine gun pinning his unit to a position, a fight where he was outnumbered, or an argument he truly believed in. But the sights, smells, and sounds inside the walls of the rehabilitation center made him want to get the hell out of the facility faster than a cat with its tail on fire.

But he couldn't leave. Not yet. This was graduation day for Reaper, aka Cory Nipton, his best friend and former teammate on SEAL Team 10. Reaper was being released from the rehabilitation center after enduring something even tougher than BUD/s training, the twenty-four week Basic Underwater Demolition/SEAL training designed to weed out the true SEALs from the wannabes.

But Reaper's release from rehab wasn't the only event that brought Tuck there that day. He was going to a wedding. His heart twisted, his palms grew clammy, and he clutched the ring box in his left hand as regret warred with guilt, creating a vile taste in his mouth.

Reaper was marrying Delaney, the only woman Tuck had ever trusted with his heart. The only woman who'd forced him to get over his past and dare to dream of a future. She was the woman he could see himself spending the rest of his life with. And today she was promising to love, honor, and cherish his best friend—a better man than Tuck by far. A hero who'd lost his right arm because Tuck hadn't given him sufficient cover. Cory deserved all the happiness he could get after being medically discharged out of the only family he'd ever known. The Navy SEALs.

His hand on the door to the room where the wedding was to take place, Tuck squared his shoulders and stepped into his future.

*Two months earlier*

Tuck glanced to his left and right. The members of Strike Force Dragon sat or stood, tense, holding onto whatever they could as the MH-60M Black Hawk dipped into the valley between two hilltops, less than a click away from the dark, quiet village. The only thing different about this mission was that, since the one before, he'd slept with the Pilot in Command of the helicopter.

Most men knew her as Razor, the call sign they used for the only female pilot flying infiltration and extraction missions for the 160th Special Operations Aviation Regiment (SOAR), Army Captain Delaney O'Connell.

Through his NVGs he picked up the bright green signature of a lookout on top of one of the buildings.

Within seconds, shots were fired at them, tracer rounds flaring in the dark. The helicopter remained just out of range of the man's rifle shots, but it wouldn't be long before a Taliban machine gunner with long-range capability was alerted with the potential of lobbing rocket-propelled grenades their way.

Wasting no time, the helicopter sank to a level just above the drop zone (DZ). While it hovered the men fast-roped down.

As soon as his boots hit the ground, Tuck brought up his M4A1 in the ready position and ran toward the sniper on the rooftop, zigzagging to avoid being locked in the enemy crosshairs.

Reaper, Big Bird, Gator, Fish, and Dustman spread out to the sides and followed.

When they were in range, Reaper took a knee and employed his uncanny ability as a sharpshooter to knock off the sentry on the rooftop.

The team continued forward into the walled town, going from building to building, until they reached the one they were after. In the center of the compound, high walls surrounded one particular brick and mud structure.

Big Bird bent and cupped his hands.

Tuck planted his boot in the man's massive paws and, with Big Bird's help, launched himself to the top of the wall, dropping down on the other side in a crouch. Weapon pointing at the building, finger on the trigger, Tuck scanned the courtyard for potential threat. People moved past windows inside. So far, no one had stepped outside to check out the disturbance. Only a matter of time. "Clear," he said into his headset.

As Dustman topped the wall, a man emerged from the side of the structure and fired on them.

Without hesitation, Tuck fired off a silent round, downing the man with one bullet.

Dustman dropped to the ground beside him and gave him a thumbs up, taking the position by the wall so Tuck could move to the corner where the dead man lay.

As they'd discussed in the operations briefing, they only had three minutes to get into the compound, retrieve their target, and get out. Kill anyone in the way, but bring out the target alive.

Once four of the six-man team were inside the wall, they breached the doorway and entered, moving from room to room. If someone or something moved, they had only a millisecond to decide whether or not to shoot.

Tuck opened the first room. Inside, small green heat signatures glowed in his NVGs. Children sleeping on mats on the floor. He eased shut the door, jamming a wedge in the gap to keep them from getting out too soon.

He moved on to the next room. When he opened the door, a woman rose from a pallet, wearing a long black burka. When she lifted her hand like she held a gun, Tuck fired, taking her down before she could pull the trigger.

As he continued in the lead position down the narrow hallway, Tuck's adrenaline hammered blood through his veins and honed his senses. His wits in hyper-alert status, his finger rested a hair's breadth away from again pulling the trigger. This was the life he was made for. Defending his country, seeking out his enemies and destroying them with a swift, deadly strike. His job was risky, dangerous, and deadly.

A man emerged from a room down the hall.

Tuck's nerves spiked. He had only a fraction of a second to identify him.

Not his target.

He pulled the trigger and nailed him with another silent round. The man slumped to the floor, his cry for help nothing more than a startled gasp.

The door he'd emerged from flew open and men bearing guns poured out.

Tuck spoke quietly into his headset. "Get down." He didn't bother to look back. His team would follow his orders without hesitation. He dropped with them, his M4A1 in front of him, and fired at the kneecaps of the men filling the hallway.

One by one, they went down, discharging their weapons, the bullets going wide and high.

In Pashto, the language spoken by most of the population of Afghanistan and Pakistan, Tuck told them to lay down their weapons.

When one of the injured enemies sat up and took aim, Tuck fired another round, putting him out of the game.

The injured enemy soldiers threw down

their guns.

"Gator, clean up out here," Tuck whispered into his mic. "Reaper and Big Bird, you're with me."

In the lead, Tuck stepped around the fallen Taliban and entered the room in a low crouch, ducking to the right. Nothing moved. Another door led into yet another unknown space. Tuck dove into the room and rolled to the side, weapon up.

As he entered, a man with an AK47 fired off a burst of rounds that whizzed past Tuck's ears, missing him, but not by much. The man shouted for Tuck to drop his weapon.

Tuck fired at the shooter's chest. He fell to the ground, revealing the man he'd been protecting. Their target, the Taliban leader they'd been briefed on. He stood straight, a pistol aimed at Tuck.

Though he wanted to pull the trigger, Tuck couldn't shoot. His mission was to bring him out alive.

His hesitation cost him. A round, fired pointblank, hit him in the chest and flung him backward to land on his ass. If not for the armor plate protecting him, he'd be a dead man. He lay still for a moment, struggling to regulate his breathing.

Reaper used the stun gun, firing off a round that hit dead on and had the man flat on his back and twitching in seconds. "You okay?" He extended his hand to help Tuck to his feet.

"Yeah." Tuck motioned to Big Bird. "Take him."

The biggest, strongest man of the team, Big Bird lifted their target and flung him over his shoulder.

Still fighting to catch his breath, Tuck led the way back to the fence. Once outside the building, he scanned his surroundings and then checked back up at the top of the roof. No signs of enemy snipers. But that didn't mean they were in the clear. They still had to navigate their way out of town and get back to the helicopter.

Leading the way, with Gator and Fish guarding the rear, Tuck hurried back along the narrow street to the outer walls of the village where the helicopter hovered nearby, waiting for their signal.

Tuck blinked the flashlight outfitted with a red lens at the hovering aircraft and it moved in, setting down for the briefest of moments, enough to get the six-man team inside. He reached over the back of the seat to the pilot and shouted, "Go!"

The Black Hawk lurched into the air, rising up and moving forward at the same time, hurrying to gain as much altitude as possible as they disappeared into the night sky, out of enemy sight and weapons range.

Not until they were well out of reach did Tuck release the breath he'd been holding and take stock of his team and their prisoner. All of them made it out alive and intact. That's the way he liked it. He'd been the only one who would have sustained injury if he hadn't been equipped with armor plating.

The co-pilot handed Tuck an aviation headset and he slipped it on.

"Nine minutes, twenty-five seconds." Gunnery Sergeant Sullivan's raspy voice sounded in Tuck's ear. "Better, but still not fast enough."

This had been a training mission, one they'd repeated five times in the past two weeks. Someone wanted them to get it right. The team was improving, but still needed to be quieter, faster, and more aware when the mission was real. The people they'd shot tonight had only been tagged with lasers. If this mission went live, the ammunition used against them would be live rounds.

Leaning back, Tuck held up nine fingers for his team to see and understand the repercussions of wearing out their welcome in a Taliban-held village.

The men nodded. Noise from the rotors precluded talking inside the chopper. When they got back to the base at Little Creek,

Virginia, they'd debrief before being dismissed for the night and hitting the club.

They'd played the same scenario five times, improving with each iteration. All six members of the team were highly skilled Navy SEALs. The cream of the crop, the most highly disciplined officers and enlisted men from the Navy.

Like Tuck, the team was tired of playing pretend. They wanted to get in and do the job. But, like most missions, they didn't know when they would go, who their target would be, or where they'd have to go to take him out. Only time and their commanding officers would tell. Only when they were about two hours out would they get their final orders and all the details.

In the meantime, they'd be off duty until the following morning's PT, unless orders came in that night. It happened. But if Tuck waited around his apartment for it to come about, he'd go stir-crazy. Besides, he wanted to see O'Connell and pick up where they'd left off the night before.

Back at base, Delaney O'Connell climbed out of the pilot's seat and grabbed her flight bag. Adrenaline still thrumming through her veins, she knew going back to her apartment for the night wasn't an option.

Her co-pilot, Lt. Mark Doggett, aka K-

9, fell in step beside her. "The team's headed to DD's Corral for a beer and some dancing. I know you don't usually like to hang out, but it's been a tough week. Wanna go?"

"Sure," she said, a little too quickly. Any other time, she'd have cut him off with a quick, but polite, *no.* But if she went back to her apartment alone, Tuck might show up and what good would that bring? Somehow, she'd fallen off the abstinence wagon with a vengeance and she was having a hard time getting back on.

"Great." K-9 cleared his throat. "Do you need a ride?"

"No, thank you. I prefer to drive myself."

"Probably a good idea. These Navy guys work hard and play harder."

As well she knew. Tuck had played her in bed like a musician played an electric guitar, hitting every one of her chords like a master.

Her body quivered with remembered excitement, her core heating to combustible levels. Maybe going to the club was a bad idea. If Tuck was there...

She squared her shoulders. They didn't call her Razor for nothing. She would cut him off like she'd done so many others who'd tried getting too close. And soon. Walking away from a physical relationship was a hell of a lot easier than walking away from an emotionally involved one. Delaney refused to invest her emotions in another man with an addiction to adrenaline rushes. She'd been there once and would not go there again.

Before Tuck, she'd gone two years without a man in her life. Two years since Mad Max, Captain Chase Madden, bought it on a leadership interdiction mission in Pakistan. When a Special Forces soldier had been left behind, he'd gone back into hostile territory against his commanding officer's order. His helicopter had been shot down. Max had been injured, but was still alive until the Taliban found him and dragged him through the streets tied to the back of a truck. By the time they untied him, he'd bled out.

Delaney had been devastated. No one knew she and Mad Max had gotten engaged two weeks prior to his deployment. And no one would, if she could help it. Being a part of the 160th Special Operations Aviation Regiment was an honor she took very seriously.

She understood her position was precarious. On more than one occasion, her CO had told her she was on probation as the only female ever entrusted with the honor of flight leader in an all-male corps. The powers that be were watching her every move. One misstep and she would be out, and she'd worked too damned hard to get here. Three years of training, and working her way up the food chain, and a rock-hard body, at least where it counted, had gotten her noticed.

Fooling around with Tuck, one of the Navy SEALs assigned to this training mission, wouldn't go over well with her commander. But the strain of anticipation and the long bout of celibacy had taken their toll on Delaney. She'd needed a release. When Tuck and Reaper offered to help her change her flat tire, she never dreamed she'd end up in bed with one of them. But those damned SEALs with their massive biceps and quads...

Holy shit. What a mistake. And Tuck would probably think their liaison meant something.

Which it didn't.

She didn't need a man in her life. Not when her missions were as dangerous as they were. And a relationship with a SEAL was as dumb as it got. Her in the Army, him in the Navy. Both deployable at a moment's notice and most likely to opposite ends of the earth. Only Kismet was what brought them together at Little Creek, Virginia, to train for a possible mission. If they deployed together, their sleeping together would only complicate matters. And she needed a clear head to complete the missions she would be responsible for flying.

Tonight, she'd tell Tuck not to expect anything. She wasn't into commitment or the long-term                    relationships.

# Other Titles by Elle James

# Other Titles by Elle James

***Cajun Magic Series***
Voodoo on the Bayou (#1)
Voodoo for Two ( #2)
Déjà Voodoo (#3)
***Stealth Operations Specialists Series***
Blown Away
Alaskan Fantasy
Nick of Time
Deadly Engagement
Deadly Liaisons
Deadly Allure
***Others***
Beneath the Texas Moon
Dakota Meltdown
Lakota Baby
Cowboy Sanctuary
Texas-Sized Secrets
Under Suspicion, with Child
Baby Bling
An Unexpected Clue
Operation XOXO
Killer Body
Bundle of Trouble
Haunted
Time Raiders: The Whisper
Cowboy Brigade
Engaged with the Boss
Tarzan & Janine
The Billionaire Husband Test

Made in the USA
San Bernardino, CA
09 March 2016